Tomas' Children

A Novel

Susan M. Szurek

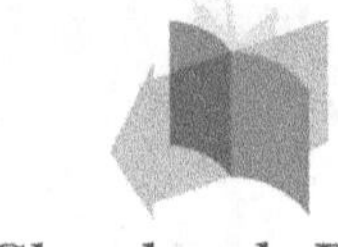

Chapbook Press

Schuler Books
2660 28th Street SE
Grand Rapids, MI 49512
(616) 942-7330
www.schulerbooks.com

Tomas'Children

ISBN 13: 9781948237970

eBook ISBN: 9781948237987

Library of Congress Control Number: 2021925521 (Paperback edition)

Copyright © 2021 Susan Szurek

The tools pictured on the cover belonged to Walter Szurek (1920-2004) and his father, Maciej Szurek (1886-1928).

Printed in the United States by Chapbook Press.

Also by Susan M. Szurek

Everstille: A Novel

Everstille's Librarian

Olivia from Everstille

Every moment I shape my destiny
with a chisel –
I am the carpenter of my own soul.

—Rumi, 13th C. Poet/Mystic

Prologue

As Tomas watched his third child come into the world accompanied by screams and blood and puke, he wondered whether he should drown it in the same manner his father used to drown the kittens on the farm.

When he was young, the barn cat had crawled into the corner of the kitchen to bring forth a mass of wet, mewing blind creatures. She had been allowed into the house because she was a good mouser, and the cold brought in those creatures. When Tomas' father found the litter, he scooped the lot of them up with an old flattened box he kept for clean-up and shoved them into a sack. He tightened the top and turned to his watching six-year-old son. "Here, go to the stream and hold this under until there's no movement or sound. Then throw them into the heap for burning."

Tomas looked at the bag, retreated one step, and shook his head. The father, not one for wasted words or sentiments, looked at Tomas, hit him on the side of his head, and did the deed himself. It wasn't the last time the task was demanded. When the dog, Molly, had a litter the next summer, the father called Tomas over again to the side of the barn. "Look there," he pointed, "Them three are fine. This one here is the runt, and she won't feed it. If you don't take and get rid of it, it'll die anyway and suffer." He scooped the runt up, grabbed an old sack and thrust the animal in it. "Go on now. Drown it, and be fast about it."

Tomas took the sack and walked towards the stream. Before he got there, he found a soft spot under a tree, pulled some leaves together and made a bed for the runt. He was going to return later and try to feed it, but the father kept him busy doing late summer chores, and he was delayed in getting back to the spot. The next morning, he found the runt partly chewed up by some animal hungry for soft meat. Tomas kicked some leaves over the remains and went back to the barn to complete his given tasks. He figured the father had been right. Save the pain and suffering by providing an early death.

The father was not a waster. He believed in quick action with a minimum of work. When Tomas went to school and learned about Thomas Jefferson and Thomas Paine in his history book, and later when told the *Bible* story about Doubting Thomas and having read the Sunday School tract for himself, he noted the missing letter in his name, and asked the father about it. "Can't hear the letter. Why use it?" was the explanation given. Later, when Tomas left the farm and set off for his own life, he took back the letter of which he had been deprived and spelled his name *Thomas* from then on.

It didn't matter to the father who he left lying in the bed at the farm, moaning with his final breaths as the cancer finished its job, looking at his son, begging for an end without suffering further. Tomas considered him, thinking of the dozens of drowned kittens and runts over the years; remembering the last dog he had, the last Molly. He looked at the man he had lived with for years and felt empty. There was no anger, no gratitude, no spite, no hope. Tomas looked around at the bedroom which was crowded with the deathbed, the casket, the dresser. Being taught not to waste emotion, Tomas reached into the back-dresser drawer where he knew the father kept his hidden money, pulled it out, placed it in his pocket, picked up the worn satchel, and left without a word

He gathered items he thought he would need and packed the satchel. He made a bedroll using blankets and placed his three books and some tools in the middle, tying it with rope, ensuring things would not fall out. An old knapsack held additional tools, a few kitchen items, some leftover cornbread, jerky, apples from the tree in the back. He walked to the porch and placed his belongings on the bottom step so he could free the chickens and horse. He opened gates and cages, allowing them to fend for themselves or to be found by neighbors. He filled the feeders with whatever he could find and wished them luck.

He gathered the packed belongings and proceeded to the wooded area to check that Molly's grave was undisturbed. He walked to the copse of trees underneath which his mother and siblings were buried, looked at the graves, bent over to remove the leaves and weeds grown around the stones. He did the task without feelings; they been expended years before. He stood up, stretched his back, and looked once more at the house where he thought he could hear, faintly, hazily, feebly, his name being called. He ignored it. Arranging the necessary items on his back, making sure his three books were safe, throwing his old jacket over a shoulder, he grabbed the full satchel and stood up.

Tomas walked past the outbuilding, the woodshop, and he paused, but decided he could not manage additional tools. He moved towards the main road which split into two: one leading south to the town past the schoolhouse, church, and small businesses struggling to succeed, and the other north away from the town, to unknown places, new circumstances, strange locales. He turned north and began his journey.

Chapter 1   Late Summer, 1918

I almost went back. I turned north on the road and walked about one hundred feet and stopped. I was far from the bedroom, the porch, and path, but I swear I heard his moans and cries. I thought he yelled my name even though I knew he barely had the strength to whisper. I knew his shotgun was on the dresser because he placed it there a month ago, saying it was loaded and ready, but I ignored it. If he wanted to use it on himself, I wouldn't stop him, but I would not shoot him like he shot Molly, even if he deserved it. He had refused all my help except for the past couple weeks, and then only because he feared he would piss the bed like a baby. Even when I helped, he chided me, told me I should be working harder, doing better, refusing to speak about anything of importance. He was dying, and I wanted him to answer my questions. I wanted to know about my mother, and my twin brother, and the other brothers, things he never told me, questions he had refused to answer, but he just looked at me and sneered. He would die in that bed in a day or two, unless he gathered strength and courage and used the gun. Either way, I would never know. I would be gone. I stood still for a minute, then readjusted my belongings and continued to walk.

I had no idea where I was headed. I knew that I could find the city of Champaign if I turned around and went the opposite way. I considered going there. My Aunt Jennifer and Uncle David had moved there some years ago. For a few years, Christmas days were spent with them at their place, although my father complained about it the entire time he drove there and back. Uncle David had started a business in the city, but I didn't know what it was. I was confident he would help me get a job. Aunt Jennifer would make him do that. There was also a chance of getting a high school diploma, just like Mr. Jensen told me I could, but I hadn't even gotten the eighth-grade certificate, so I didn't know how that would work. There was something in me, a stubbornness my father said I had, that made me travel a different way, away from what I had known, into a different place where I could meet new people. I continued the northward direction.

Parts of the road I traveled on were familiar. I had left the town of Levett, where I grew up, but some of the farmland was known to me. I knew some of the farmhouses I was passing contained a bedframe or a bookcase or a table that my father and I had produced in the woodshop. I remembered traveling to this area and delivering some of the items. I wondered how they were holding up, if they needed any repairs or re-staining. I was sure I could do that, and it would be a way to earn money. But I couldn't just go to the door and knock. There would be questions about my father, and why I was alone, and where I was going. It was too risky, so I forgot that idea and just continued to walk.

I kept to the main road but over to the side; not that there were too many travelers down this way, but a couple automobiles and a horse and wagon had driven by. They hadn't seen me. When I heard their noise, I walked into the field and sat low until they passed. I was nervous and anxious. I doubted if anyone who knew me would actually come this way, but I didn't want to have to answer questions or give explanations. I kept walking until the heat beat down around me, warming my head until I took off my cap and pushed my sweaty hair back. I decided to find a tree and rest and eat some of the cornbread I packed, along with some sips from the jar of water in the knapsack.

As I rested, I began to think through my plan. Or rather, lack of one. I wasn't sure where I would spend the night or, after the food I had with me was gone, what I would eat. In my hurry to leave, to get away from the farm, I hadn't planned for all consequences. I was unafraid to sleep in the woods or to be alone, but lack of food and water had me worried. Once I reached a town, I knew I could buy some supplies, but until then, I had to ration what I had. After sitting for a while, I took stock of my supplies and thought I could last a day or two with what I had, if I were careful.

Looking around to make sure no one was spying on me, although I couldn't imagine who would be in this wooded place, I took out the money I had pocketed and brought with me and decided to count it. Some was my own saved cash. That was three dollars and some change. Together, with the cash I took from the dresser, I had twenty-two dollars and eighteen cents. Most of it was single dollars although I had one five-dollar bill, and it sure seemed like a lot. Because buying supplies for the farm and the woodshop had been one of my duties, I knew some of the costs of foodstuffs at the Nelson General Store, but wasn't sure if things would cost the same in other stores and different towns. I looked at my money and thought about what my father had once said: "Don't keep all your money in one place. Spread it around in hiding spots. If a thief comes, he is likely to only get some of it." I divided the money up, putting some in the books in the bedroll, some in the bottom of the knapsack, and secreted more in the satchel, in the pocket of the other pair of pants I packed. I left the change and two dollars in my pocket and thought I was being smart. Then I thought back to the advice and felt stupid. What made me think this was the only money my father had? He was sure to have taken his own advice, and there had to be more cash hidden away in the farmhouse. I never looked. Wasn't going back now, and didn't think the hidden cash would do him much good anyway. I wondered if whoever found my father's body would also find his money.

I decided to continue walking and get as far as possible before I needed to find a spot to sleep for the night, so I got up and readjusted my belongings, and started out again. There was a breeze, and I was grateful for it because although it was the second week of September, it was still summer-warm. I kept changing the satchel from hand to hand and began to wonder why I had packed it. There were some clothes and an old towel and a few things I just threw in, not knowing what I would need, but it was heavy. I wondered how much room I had in the knapsack and the bedroll. Maybe I could fit the items in them and leave the satchel. But, if I carried the satchel into a town, I might be able to sell it and get some money for it. Probably not much, but it was in decent shape and I hated to just leave it. In the morning, I would try to rearrange everything and empty it which would make for easier carrying.

My feet were starting to hurt, and I was getting hungry and tired. I didn't recognize the farmhouses I was passing, so I was sure this was an area where I knew no one. And no one would know me. I thought it was time to look for a place to spend the night. If I could find a stream, I would be able to refill my water jar and splash some cold water on my face. What would it cost to rent a room in a hotel should there be one in the next town? I had never been in one, but the thought of a bed and some warm water sounded inviting. I wasn't sure I could afford that pleasure. Tonight, I would find a soft spot under a tree and make my own hotel. I walked on and noted that the farmhouses seemed closer together and figured that meant I was near to a town. Wasn't sure how far I had traveled, but thought at least fifteen miles. I hadn't stopped for any length of time except for a lunch break, and I had kept a good pace. Time to look for a spot.

Up ahead there were a couple of farmhouses. I considered going to one and asking for a drink from the well and if I could stay in their barn, but I was still travel-shy and worried about strangers. I noted where I was and looked towards the east where I could see a small wooded spot, and I headed towards it. As I crossed over to the trees, I saw some autumn berry bushes, and taking my cap, I filled it with as many as I could and stuffed my mouth with the juiciness. September was the season for them, and I was glad to find something to add to my meager dinner. I took the capful and walked into the trees and looked around for a place to make my bed.

I found a spot and checked it out for poison ivy. I knew the leaves were probably dropped, but the stems could still give a bad itch. I also looked for snake-holes, and once it all seemed clear, I set up my bedroll and secured my belongings behind me. Tomorrow I would need to look for a stream or a friendly farmer's well, but tonight I would need to make do with the food I allotted myself and the remaining water from the jar. I was grateful for the berries and saved half of them for morning breakfast. No coffee and eggs then. That made me think that I should have hard-boiled some eggs to bring with me. I felt stupid again.

I ate slowly, thinking about what I would do tomorrow, hoping I would find a small town to refill supplies, and wondering about my future. I took out the Sherlock Holmes book Mr. Jensen had given me and was able to reread one of the stories before it became too dark to see the words. This was the book into which he had written his address in Champaign, and I wondered if he were married now, if he still taught school, and I supposed I would never know. I could write him, but what would be the use of that? I wasn't sure he would even remember me; after all, it was over two years ago he left.

I gathered the blanket around me and settled back. The tree was sturdy, and the rustling leaves were soothing. I looked upwards where a few stars were starting to show and wondered if my father was dead yet. I guess I should have felt sadder than I did, but I had made up my mind and chosen my path. Tomorrow I would, with luck, find a town, get some supplies, and maybe sell the satchel. Beyond that, I wasn't sure what the future held. As I drifted off, as I fell asleep under the tree and the leaves and the stars, I remembered this day was my birthday. I was sixteen.

***

Eventually, and quickly, my travel-shyness disappeared. The first town I visited didn't have a hotel, so I spent no money there, but I did buy some supplies at the general store in town and was able to sell the satchel for seventy-five cents. I entered the town's one small restaurant during the late afternoon when it was not busy, and spent thirty-five cents from the sale of the satchel.

I had only eaten in a restaurant a few times, so I was nervous about ordering, but the advertised special seemed the best thing to get.

The plate came with meatloaf, mashed potatoes, gravy, beets, and bread and butter. After the little I had to eat the day before, it all tasted great. I also got something called *rice pudding* which was smooth and sweet. I drank plenty of water, and the waitress kept filling up the coffee cup. Afterwards, I asked to use their bathroom and stayed in it for a time, doing what was needed, but also washing up the best I could. The waitress looked at me strangely when I came out. Probably because my hair was wet. I tried to wash it in the small sink, but I just thanked her, waved, and left with all my belongings on my back.

Traveling became easier after that. I figured things out, and the more I traveled, the gutsier I became. The first time I decided to knock on a farmhouse and ask to fill up my water jar, the woman was kind and offered to make me a sandwich. I was grateful for her offer, and when I left, she gave me another and some cookies she had been baking. I think it was because of the story I told her.

I pride myself on not being a liar. But I was always being asked who I was, why I was alone, where was my family, and what was my background, so I came up with answers. The story I first told seemed to work, so I stuck to it. That first woman I spoke to, the one who gave me the sandwiches and cookies, asked those questions, and I felt that I needed to tell her anything but the truth. I told her I was leaving the farm my brother owned because he was joining the army. I was traveling north to Chicago to live with my sister and her husband. I would be finishing high school in the city. Sometimes I changed the details. My grandfather had died and my mother sent me to Detroit to obtain my inheritance. My mother had sent me to live with her aunt who had recently died, and now I was going home to northern Illinois. Or, my sister met and married a circus performer when the circus came through our town, and I didn't want to have to clean after the elephants, so I was traveling to stay with my uncle who was a famous writer. I admit that last story was used only once. The woman I told it to just looked sideways at me and told me I needed to get going. She didn't give me a sandwich either.

The fall weather was perfect for my traveling. I slept in barns when I could and in the wooded areas otherwise. There were ponds and small waters I would swim and bathe in until the weather turned. I took rides with farmers who offered them, happily climbing on the back of the wagons. Sometimes I caught a ride in an automobile with a traveling salesman. I stopped at small towns and refilled my supplies, and I periodically needed to sell off some of the extra clothes I had packed, but that simply made my load lighter. September and October passed, and there was some early November rain. My money was slowly disappearing, and soon the snow would come, and what would happen then? A job was needed.

I found myself in Livingston County in a place called Newtown which was a larger town than most of the others I had passed through, and the main street was filled with more businesses than just the usual general store and hardware store. I thought that I would be able to find a job here, earn some money, and find someplace to stay. I counted my remaining money and had less than eight dollars left. It was cold; November was taking hold, and a decision needed to be made. I walked around the town and caught a glimpse of myself in a store window. I looked dirty and unkempt, and I wouldn't hire myself looking like this, so I spent some of my money.

I had not yet stayed at any hotel, but thought it was time. And the Newtown Hotel had a sign in the window listing prices. I could share a room without a private bathroom for one dollar. The shared bathroom was down the hall, and when I checked in, I was the only one in the room. I was told that I would probably get a roommate, but if no one checked in, the room would be mine for the night. I agreed and signed the hotel register with my new name: Thomas Allerton. I now spelled it with the *h*, just like Thomas Jefferson had. I asked a few questions, took the room key, and walked up the stairs to the room on the third floor in the back. There were two beds, a small table and chair, and a small dresser. I put my belongings underneath the far bed, placed my old towel on the bed to claim it, and left the room with the remainder of my money and the key in my pocket.

There was a barber shop down one street, and I walked in. Before I sat down, I asked about the price. A haircut was thirty-five cents and a shave was fifteen cents. I felt the fuzz along my chin and decided I needed both, so I handed over the money and, for the first time in my life, had a real haircut with a real barber. This was different than having my father chop off my hair or trying to do it myself. I was feeling grown, and asked the barber about job availabilities in the town.

"Well, what can you do?" he inquired.

"I spent years as an apprentice to a carpenter, and I know that trade."

"Years? Hmmm," he said, looking at my now clean shaven and sixteen-year-old face. "James Turner is the carpenter and furniture maker in town. Not sure he is looking, but his shop is down two blocks on Hudson Street. Turn right when you get there."

I thanked the man, tipped him a nickel although I couldn't spare it, and left. It was late afternoon, and I took a walk down two streets and over to the right to find the shop. I didn't plan on going in at this time, but thought the morning, mid-morning, would be better. First, I needed to get back to the hotel and get to the shared third-floor bathroom for a good cleaning. I had a semi-clean shirt, the only other one I had because I had sold off most of my clothes. I would wear it tomorrow. Walking back to the hotel, I asked the man at the front desk if someone else had checked into my room, but he shook his head. I started up the stairs.

It felt good that night, to bathe and then sleep in a bed. I didn't eat out, but snacked on the apples and crackers I had in my knapsack. I had already spent too much of my dwindling cash, and if I couldn't get a job, I wasn't sure what I would do, so I drank some water, went to bed early, and, I swear, as soon as I laid down, and my newly cut head of hair landed on the flatten pillow, I was asleep.

I felt great the following morning although I was hungry. The sleep cleared my head, and I readied myself for the day. I didn't have a comb, but thought my hair looked fine and brushed it with my fingers. I was clean, and my shirt looked good even though I could tell it wouldn't fit too much longer. I had grown in the past months. I wiped my boots with the old towel I had and used it to sponge some dirt off my jacket. I placed my cap on my head at what I thought was a jaunty angle, and examining myself in the cracked and wavy mirror over the dresser, thought I looked fine. At least seventeen-years-old. I packed up everything, re-rolled my knapsack with the tools and the books, and mounted it all on my back. Taking my time, I walked down the stairs, gave my room key to the man at the front desk and headed towards Hudson Street

Thinking back on that day, luck must have been with me. I didn't find out until later, but James Turner, furniture maker and carpenter for the city of Newtown, Illinois had just received a large order for additional furniture from one of the wealthiest families in the area. While he couldn't afford to turn it down, he wasn't sure how he would complete the order by himself. I watched him read some papers through the window from the outside of his shop. Then I stored my belongings to the side of the building underneath a staircase, took a deep breath, pushed open the door, and walked in.

Chapter 2   1915 – 1918

    In the fall of 1915, Tomas turned thirteen and was finished with school. That is what his father told him the previous spring when he completed sixth grade. Before the fall term began, the teacher at Levett's school came to the farm and spoke with the father to convince him to allow Tomas to complete the last two years of school. He didn't mention that there was a possibility of Tomas obtaining a high school diploma from a high school in the city of Champaign because he was going to save that argument for the following year. But the father did not allow Tomas to return to school. When the teacher visited a second time, the father was rude and short, and at the third attempt, he grabbed his shotgun, pointed it at the teacher, and told him that if he appeared again, it would be used. He did not appear again.

    The teacher circumvented the father's refusal to allow his son additional education. He loaned Tomas books from his personal library and strategized a way to continue meeting and discussing them. The father did not attend church, but Tomas did since it allowed him to get away from the farm for a brief time. While the father did not encourage a belief in a deity, he didn't stop his son, assuming he would soon tire of walking all that way just to listen to nonsense. Tomas attended Sunday services so that he and the teacher could meet before and after for their discussions. The discussions were abridged, and it was not an ideal plan, and the winter weather made it difficult to meet on a regular basis. But Tomas, whose life was monotonous and demanding, looked forward to the conversations.

    In the summer of 1916 when Tomas was almost fourteen, he met with the teacher one last time and learned that he would be leaving to take another position at a school in Champaign. It was a good appointment, offering additional money, and allowing him to be closer to his fiancée. He gave Tomas three volumes. "These will be the start of your own library. I am only sorry we won't be able to discuss them, but I have included my new address in the first one, and I do hope that one day you will be able to visit." Tomas looked at the books: *Lord Jim, The Tempest, The Return of Sherlock Holmes*, and thanked the teacher for his thoughtfulness, wished him the best of luck, shook his hand, and never saw him again.

    In the early spring of 1917, Tomas was given a new task. On a biweekly basis, he drove the wagon into town to pick up needed supplies for the kitchen and woodshop. He enjoyed listening to the talk of the men in Nelson's General Store, and Burt's Feed and Hardware Store. During one of his trips, the group was discussing President Wilson's second term, the Great War, and the newly passed conscription law.

"Son, you are lucky to be so young," said one of the men in the general store as he looked at Tomas, "My sister's boy is facing army time now. Sad state we are in," and he shook his head.

Mr. Nelson filled Tomas' sack with the cornmeal and other items, and as Tomas passed over the money, he said, "Yep, Tomas, good thing your Pa still has you at home. How is he doin'?"

"Fine, Sir," answered Tomas, even though he knew this was not the truth. He gathered his change and the sack and left to travel back to the farm, planning to drive slowly in order to enjoy his bit of autonomy.

By the fall of 1917 when Tomas was fifteen and taller than his father, he had taken over most of the work on the farm and in the woodshop. His father, never talkative or friendly became even more isolated and withdrawn, except for those times he rebuked Tomas and chided him for what he saw as insufficient diligence. Tomas had learned over the years to maintain his silence and lower his head during these scoldings. He hadn't received any of the head thumps the father would regularly dispatch when he was younger and had no intention of encouraging their reappearance. Tomas remained silent.

As the year progressed, he saw less of his father and completed more of the work. He was absorbed, during the pinch of free time he had, in reading and rereading the three books given him by the teacher. During decent weather, he would get the dog, Molly, and they would walk the wooded area. Tomas looked for specific timber pieces to gather for his carving and whittling when the winter settled in, and those activities were the only diversions he had from his required work. He no longer went to Sunday services because there were no more discussions, and, just as the father suspected, he was tired of listening to the opining of the preacher and his expatiation about sin.

And then there was the father. During the late fall of 1917, he mentioned that he needed to go to town to take care of some *business*, but would return soon, and Tomas should complete his assigned tasks. He was gone for the better part of the day, and when he came home, he stopped the wagon, called to Tomas, told him to take care of the horse, and went into his bedroom. Tomas did as he was told and then continued working in the woodshop alone. When it was darkening and the father hadn't come out to the building, Tomas decided to end for the day and went into the house. It was gloomy and quiet in the dusk, and no supper had been started, so he began to make cornbread to eat with the leftover stew which he heated up. His father's bedroom door was still closed. When Tomas had supper ready, he called out to his father, but there was no answer. He walked over to the door and knocked, telling him supper was ready. After a few seconds, the father growled, "Not hungry," and Tomas ate by himself, wondering what had happened.

For the next week or so, the father was rarely seen. He appeared in the woodshop a few times to watch what Tomas was doing, and except for some dispassionate comments, ignored him. Once or twice, he ate dinner with Tomas who made it after he finished work, but other than coming out to get a cup of coffee at breakfast, Tomas didn't see the father. It was not until the weather had turned, and the trees were mostly nude that he discovered what the business in town concerned.

Early one nippy morning, Tomas woke, started breakfast, and completed the morning chores. When he glanced out to the woodshop, he noticed light and movement. He finished watering and feeding the chickens and set the egg basket in the kitchen before he walked out to investigate. The father was inside hauling planks of white oak onto the work table, busy making something. When he saw Tomas watching him, he put the ruler and marking gauge down and stood looking at the planks.

"What are you making? I'm getting coffee and breakfast made and then can come out here to help. I didn't know we had another order," and Tomas watched the father.

"Making a casket," said the father.

Tomas looked around. They hadn't had a call for a casket in over a year, and there remained one small child's casket in the corner. He wasn't aware of any recent deaths, and obviously this casket was for an adult. He asked the question to which he suspected he knew the answer.

"For who?"

The father looked directly at his son, and as he did, Tomas saw the quick aging, the ebbing coloring, the effaced weight, and the palpable pain he hadn't before.

"It's mine. Go on back and get breakfast. I'll be in shortly. Just want to get this measured," and the fated man turned his head, took up the ruler and gauge, and proceeded to work.

***

It was a cancer. An ugly, grisly disease whose promised torture advanced into the father's stomach and guts; eating and chewing its way. At first, it inched unhurriedly, burrowing into softness, giving feeble twists and jabs, but soon moderate spasms appeared, and finally torturous excruciations became the father's cursed companion.

During that fall of 1917, when the moderate spasms were so bothersome that the father knew there was something horribly wrong, he visited a new doctor in the next town. Levett's physician, Doctor Warin, had died several years earlier, from some strange malady. The doctor was found by his wife surrounded by some bottles and hypodermic needles. The incident was hushed up, and only fragmentary rumors were whispered about at small gatherings in Nelson's General Store, and Burt's Feed and Hardware, but the town had lost its one physician. The father had no choice, so he traveled to the next town. He waited in the unfamiliar doctor's office and was poked and prodded and questioned, and eventually, given the hopeless diagnosis and appalling news. Afterwards, he traveled back to the farm where he stayed in his bed for a week, eyeing his shotgun, periodically picking it up, deciding his destiny, and railing against what he saw as his own unmanliness. Painful survival dominated.

He did not cling to his one remaining son. He spoke, when he did, with bluntness and specificity to the subject at hand, offering no clarification and accepting no sympathy. Once the affliction was spoken of, it was never again brought up. Tomas discussed treatments and inquired about cures, but the father knew there were none available and refused to accept or extend optimism. They continued working together when the disease allowed, completing scant orders, keeping up the small farm, and waiting.

***

In the late fall of 1917, the dog, Molly, became sick with a similar disease. Tomas kept the animal warm, hand-fed her, scratched her ears, and gave her the comfort he would have extended to the father had it been allowed. She settled close to Tomas, and as he carved and whittled through the chilly evenings, the two traded warmth and shared ease. Tomas thought Molly had until spring or so, and before winter took root, they walked together whenever possible. Around the farm and through the wooded areas, Molly looped through the fallen leaves, ambling alongside Tomas, both grateful for the companionship and the time.

On an early morning, before the snow came, Tomas was in the woodshop finishing up the last order that would need to be delivered that afternoon. This was a small side table Mr. Nelson wanted for his young granddaughter's birthday gift. Tomas had also carved a delicate keepsake box to go with the table, and while no money would be exchanged, he had bartered for the foodstuffs from the general store which would get the two men through the coming winter. Tomas was in the shop, checking on one table leg, making sure it was even. After he finished this, he would eat a quick breakfast, load the gift into the wagon and drive to the general store in town. He thought that Molly, who had perked up a bit lately, would enjoy a ride with him, sitting next to him, sniffing the air, looking at the scenery, Tomas' right hand holding the reins, his left laid across Molly's back, scratching her ear. He wrapped the old blanket used to protect completed furniture around the side table, lifted it down from the workbench, and as he placed it on the floor, he heard a gunshot.

It was not unusual to hear a sporadic shot in the woods, but this one was close. It seemed to be just to the south, where the trees began to crowd together to form a fence, and Tomas was startled. He opened the door to the shop and began to walk quickly in the morning lightness, and he saw a figure approaching him. The father was carrying a shotgun.

Tomas ran towards him breathless, and asked, "What happened? What was that? Is there something wrong?"

The father stopped and looked at Tomas. The boy would be sixteen next year. He was almost six-feet tall and hadn't finished growing yet. His dark hair needed cutting, and the strength of his muscles was noticeable under the plaid shirt whose sleeves were rolled up. The boy was talented and smart; he had already surpassed the father's wood-working abilities, and in the morning sun, looked exactly like his mother, Clara. Precisely like the photograph of his dead mother which was in the dresser drawer in the bedroom. The father examined his own feelings and came to the conclusion that he loved the boy. His only child. And he hated him for his robustness and stamina and attractiveness and proficiencies.

"That dog was sick. Needed to be done. Went too long. Left it at the edge of the woods, so you can bury it or leave it for the animals to find. Up to you. Get a shovel from the shed, and when you're done, deliver that table. I'm going in," and he began to walk to the house.

Tomas grabbed the father's arm and stopped him. He pulled the man around, not much of an effort given the frailty of the man and the heartiness of the boy, and he leaned down to the ravaged face, sickness having taken length from the father.

"Why did you do that? Molly would have lived another six months. She was *my* dog, *mine*, and you had no right. I was taking care of her! You are cruel and awful, and I am glad you are sick. You deserve to be!"

The two of them glowered at each other, replies, responses, swirling around them, butting against their chests, poking holes in their souls, daring reactions. The father pulled away. He took a step back and grasped the shotgun hard, jerking it upright. There were no more words, so he turned and walked to the house and Tomas watched him, the tears he held back pouring down his cheeks, wetting his plaid shirt front. Once the man was in the house, Tomas walked to the shed and gathered a spade and shovel.

He went to the woodshop. Taking off his plaid shirt, he put his jacket on. When he got to where Molly was laying, blood soaking her fur, her eyes staring, her tongue hanging from the side of her mouth, Tomas wrapped his shirt around the animal, buttoning up the front, thinking that somehow, it would keep the dead creature warm. He found a space near a tree, where the ground was still soft, and using the tools, dug deep, deeper than necessary, and placed Molly, wearing his shirt, in the ground. He knelt, before shoveling dirt on top of her, and held his hand to her head, stroking it gently, feeling the silkiness, staying there until his legs began to ache, and he could no longer put off the burial. Tomas packed down the soil, and finding some large stones, moved them as markers on top of Molly's grave. Then he stood up, gathered his tools, and went back to the farm to deliver Mr. Nelson's granddaughter's birthday gift.

***

Tomas and the father barely spoke during the winter of 1917. When spring 1918 came, the quiet continued. However, instead of sitting in the kitchen before the warming stove, Tomas spent most of his time in the woodshop, busying himself making a bookcase one of the town families had ordered. He took his time and managed to be absent most of the day. As the weather improved, he spent time in the small truck patch, cleaning and hoeing and readying the ground for the seeds which would be planted. He cleaned the chicken coop and watched to see if any of the cats were returning. They had been ejected from the house by the father who never liked the animals although he did bring a pair of kittens to his wife once. She liked them.

The father did no work. His time was spent on the porch when he was able to sit in the old rocker, or in bed, when his pain was too great.

He had completed the building of his casket last winter before the snow set in, and it was leaning against the back wall of the woodshop. Waiting. It was the last thing he would ever make. He did all the work himself and would not ask Tomas for help, which he would not give anyway. There was the specter of a dog between them.

Now that spring had come and the weather was improved, the father needed to talk to Tomas. He needed his help. He was on the porch when the afternoon sun was waning, watching Tomas leave the shop and amble towards the house. As his son walked up the steps and reached for the door, he spoke, his voice rusty from disuse.

"Boy, I need your help."

Tomas stopped. He was tempted to walk into the house and ignore the father, but he turned and waited.

"I need your help in moving the casket from the shop."

"Move it where?"

"I want it in the bedroom with me."

Tomas almost laughed because the request was so ludicrous. But he knew the father had no sense of humor and was serious about this. He sighed and then said, "When do you want to do that?"

"Now," said the father, "I feel stronger this afternoon and am not sure what tomorrow will bring. Help me up from this rocker and let's do it now."

Tomas touched his father for the first time in years and helped him up from the seat. Together, with the assistance of the wheelbarrow and some straps, they were able to maneuver the casket into the house and through the bedroom door. The father wanted it placed at the foot of his bed where it barely fit, but they moved the dresser and managed to get it straightened out. When it was in place, the father looked at Tomas, grunted and nodded his head. Tomas left the bedroom, and the father closed the door.

Tomas made himself some dinner, not bothering to ask the father if he wanted any. He knew he would not eat. He sat by himself at the kitchen table, then cleaned up and did the evening chores. He spent the balmy evening sitting on the steps watching the path meandering from the edge of the porch to the road which traveled south and north. He thought and considered.

Chapter 3   Winter, 1918

I offered to work for free and show Mr. Turner what I could do. I was confident about my ability and knowledge, but less so about my family circumstances. When he inquired about it, asking the same questions others had asked, I gave him the truthful story. Almost the truthful story. I told him my father had died (I was sure he had by this time), leaving so many debts to others that his tools and property were auctioned off to pay the money owed, and I was left on my own at the age of eighteen. I thought that adding a couple years onto my age would increase the time I had spent as an apprentice. I also gave myself an eighth-grade certificate which I had, so I told him, unfortunately lost. James Turner accepted my story and the free offer, and told me to return the following day for work. He did ask where I was staying and I answered, "Last night, I was at the Hotel Newtown, Sir. A decent place for now, but should you accept me, I hope to find a permanent room." That he accepted I would be staying in the hotel on a nightly basis was his own assumption.

We shook hands. I told him I would be back in the morning at the eight-o'clock starting time and left. I knew he was watching me, so I turned to wave and continued walking down the street towards the Hotel Newtown. I turned the corner and walked to the back of the building, picked up my hidden belongings, and thought I would treat myself to a real breakfast with some of my dwindling money.

I found a restaurant and ate. I used their bathroom when I was finished and did my best to clean up again although I was still clean from the last night's bath. There was no way I could afford to stay at the hotel again, so I walked the town all day, picked up a few groceries at a small store, and tried to figure out where I would spend the night. A clock in the town square told me it was almost seven in the evening, and it was growing cold. Darkness was coming, and the lights which were on in the stores and businesses began to shut off as they closed for the day. I went down Hudson Street to peer at Mr. Turner's building and saw it was closed for the night, so I crossed the street. There was a staircase around the side, the same one under which I had stored my belongings, and I wanted to see where it led. I looked up. I saw no one around, so I went up the stairs and found myself on a small porch before a locked door. There was a window but no light was on, and I couldn't see in. I thought the place was empty, and the porch was tiny and exposed. I considered trying to curl up on it for the night, but it was unsafe. I needed someplace semi-enclosed. I longed for the safety and security of the trees under which I had spent so many nights.

I walked down the stairs which I noticed were rickety, and around to the back of the building. There was a door in the back, probably the door where supplies would be received. There were three steps down to it and a small framed alcove above. This was it. This is where I would spend the night, so I checked around to make sure no one was there to see me, spread out the old bedroll and blankets and tried to make myself comfortable. I ate some of the crackers and the last of the apples, drank some of the water from the jar, and made do for the night.

The sun woke me in the morning. I wondered what time it was and if I could get a breakfast and clean up a bit before I started work. I gathered everything up, walked to the front and, according to the town clock, saw it was not seven o'clock yet. I wondered if the small diner I ate at yesterday would be opened, and I went there. They opened at seven, and I was the first customer. I was watching my money, and ordered some coffee and oatmeal which was what I thought I could afford. I went to their bathroom, did what I needed to, cleaned up, and walked to Turner's building. I was early, but that allowed me to hide my things under the stairwell again and straighten my clothing out. I wished I had a clean shirt to put on and thought that once I began to earn some money, perhaps I could buy some things. My boots were not only wearing out, but my feet had grown, and they were uncomfortable. I knew shoes were expensive, but that was an expense I would need to swallow. I waited in front of the door, and just after eight o'clock, Mr. Turner drove up in his automobile. He stopped it in front and gave me a nod as he saw me waiting.

"Good morning, Mr. Turner," I called.

"Morning, Thomas," he answered. "I see you are here and ready to work. Here, will you hold this while I get the door?" and without my answer, he thrust a package into my arms.

We walked into the building and he turned on the light. He motioned for me to place the bag on the front table. "Mrs. Turner always sends too much food for lunch, and I rarely get a chance to eat it all. I hope you didn't bring a large lunch today. You can help me eat the sandwiches she packed."

I was pleased. I didn't think I would be eating until late tonight, and then I wasn't sure what I would eat or where I could get any food, so I nodded in agreement.

'Come in here," and Mr. Turner pointed to a small room in the back. "This is my office. I'm rarely in here except to do some invoices or make tea, but you can put your jacket here, and over there is a bathroom and sink," and he pointed to the door at the side, "and I keep the carpenter aprons here. I guess you don't have one, so just take one and bring me one too."

I got the aprons, slipped mine on, and immediately felt back at home, back at the woodshop, back at the farm. An unexpected lump came to my throat, and I cleared it and coughed, and handed him his apron.

"There's water in the office in a large container, and some cups are there too. As you know, carpentry is a dusty and thirst-creating business. So, help yourself. Are you ready?"

"Yes, Sir, I am."

"Then let's see what you can do."

He showed me the list of new furniture he had agreed to make, and pointed to the bookcase that had been ordered. "There, start with that. Start easy, and let me examine your work through this week. Come on back to the work room, and I'll show you where you will get what you need."

The day passed quickly. The last item I had made at the farm's woodshop was a bookcase, and while this one was larger in size, it was all familiar to me. Mr. Turner began work on a small side table, and we worked companionably throughout the day. He would stop his work and come over and watch me for a while, grunting and nodding, and commenting now and again about what I was doing. But there was no chiding or scolding me about my work. I felt comfortable and sure about what I was doing, and when we stopped for a brief break and to eat some of the sandwiches his wife had sent, he stopped chewing to speak to me.

"Seems you know what to do, Thomas. Figure we'll get the small things out of the way; the single-person jobs, and once they are done, sanded, stained, we can work together on the larger dining table and chairs we need to make. How long did you work as apprentice?"

I swallowed some water and tried to give myself some time to figure out the years I would tell him. I had started to help my father when I was six, so that was ten years, but I told him I was eighteen. Would twelve years be too much to admit to? I remembered that I told him I finished eight years of schooling, and all this math in my head was swirling around. I needed to be reasonable about my stories.

"I began working with my father at six, but of course, I was going to school, so didn't work full time. I did things after class and on weekends and summers, but really worked full time for almost four years. After my schooling that is," and I took another drink of water, hoping my math was worthy of the school ciphering awards I received.

"Hmm. You appear to have a steady hand and decent knowledge, so keep at the case and on Friday, I'll let you know about the job. Another sandwich?"

We worked through the day. I was used to working and not speaking, so the fact that Mr. Turner was a quiet man didn't bother me. A few times the front doorbell sounded, and he left to take care of a customer or talk to a friend who stopped by, and I continued to work. When the end of the day came, we cleaned up, put away the tools, took off the aprons, and I gathered my jacket. As we left, Mr. Turner offered to give me a ride to the Hotel Newtown so I wouldn't have to walk, but I assured him that walking was a good thing after a long work day. He waved me off, and I headed towards the hotel. Once I couldn't see him or his automobile, I headed back around to the building, gathered my things, and made my way to the back where I spent the night on the back steps again.

The following days passed in much the same way. Thursday came, and I was sure I had done a good job on everything I was given. It was raining at the close of the day, and Mr. Turner absolutely insisted on driving me to the hotel, so I got in the passenger seat, and he drove the few streets to my supposed sleeping place. I thanked him, got out of the auto, waved him off, and made my way into the hotel where I stood until I was sure he was gone. Rain or not, I had to get back to his building, so I turned up the collar on my jacket, lowered my cap, and took off at a fast pace, trying to dodge the rain from store awning to store awning. When I reached the building and my belongings, I just stayed under the stairwell attempting to stay as dry as possible. The rain did not let up, and I thought that I might as well stay the night where I was. I would be more protected here than on the back steps. I took the bedroll apart, placed one of the blankets over my head and around my body and attempted to make myself comfortable for the night.

I was uncomfortable all that night. Even more so than at the back stairs. It was very late when the rain stopped, and I finally fell into a fitful sleep. I woke up the next morning, much later than the past few days, with Mr. Turner kicking my toe with his shoe and calling, "Thomas, Thomas, wake up."

I opened my eyes and knew I just lost the job. He looked at me and said, "Gather your things and let's go into the shop." He waited while I tried to organize things, but eventually, because he was waiting at the opened door, I gave up and just grabbed everything and walked into the building. The only thing I was surprised at was that he even allowed me in and didn't just throw me out then. I stood holding the mess of my blankets and knapsack and cap, and waited for the yelling to start.

"Put those things down. Go into the bathroom and wash up, and then come out here."

I did as he said. I used the bathroom, washed my face and hands, tried to straighten out my clothes and slick back my hair which, because I slept so awkwardly under the stairwell, had one side which stuck up, looking like I had donkey's ears. *Perfect*, I thought, *I am a perfect ass.* I came out of the bathroom, into the office and found Mr. Turner had made tea. He handed me a cup and motioned me to sit down.

He took a sip of his tea and asked, "You weren't staying at Hotel Newtown, were you?"

"No, Sir."

"I know because I stopped there early this morning. I was going to pick you up and take you to breakfast. We were going to talk about your job."

I tried to swallow the tea and felt I was going to choke. It was over. I had less than three dollars left and no prospect of a job. I had no place to stay, no family, and I had lied about my age and education to this man. I sighed and looked down at the floor.

"Why didn't you stay at the hotel? Why did you tell me you were there? Where were you staying?"

I might as well be truthful now. It no longer mattered. "I did stay one night at the hotel, and I did it so I could take a bath and sleep in a bed and look decent when I asked you for this job. I have no money. At least very little. That night in the hotel was the first night I slept in a bed in over two months. I didn't want you to think I couldn't take care of myself, so I just let you think I was staying there. I've been spending the nights behind this building, at the back entrance. But, when it rained so hard last night, I stayed under the stairwell. I'm sorry, Mr. Turner. The fact is, I'm good at making furniture and working with wood. I have a talent for it. I need this job and want to do what I know I can. What I'm good at. What I like to do."

Mr. Turner took another sip of his tea and watched me. He put his cup down and leaned forward. "I know you have a talent. That's obvious. Let me ask about your clothes. You've worn the same shirt all week. Your shoes don't fit anymore. Do you have any other clothing?"

"No, Sir. I have grown over the past year, and have had no money to get new things. I was hoping that I could earn some and get a new shirt and maybe shoes. I do have another shirt, but it's in bad shape. Worse than this one."

There was silence and then, "What about your story? Did your father die? Was he in debt? Are you just a runaway?"

I stuck to my original story. There was only so much truth I could face. "My father is dead. We lived alone on the small farm, and it was a hard time. I left because I had no future there and no family."

More silence. Then he said, "The job pays ten dollars a week to start. I know that's not much, but this is a small town, and I will need to test you further. I own this building, and there is a small empty apartment upstairs. I'll rent it to you for two dollars a week and take the rent out of your pay, so you'll get eight dollars weekly," and then he got up and reached into his pocket and pulled out two ten-dollar bills. He handed them to me. "This is an advance on your salary. There is a decent second-hand store called Mandy's on the next street. Go there and get some clothes that fit. See if they have some boots for you. They usually have a goodly supply. I'll take an additional two dollars out of your pay for the next ten weeks which means that for ten weeks, you'll get six dollars, and eight after that. You'll have to get your own food and personal needs from that. Do you think you can manage?"

I was shocked. Apparently, I had the job. And six dollars a week was more than I could even imagine. I almost felt bad having told a story about my age and education, but kept my mouth shut. I stood up and thanked Mr. Turner and held out my hand and told him he wouldn't regret it. And I meant it. And I would keep my word for the years I would spend with him.

"Let's go up to the apartment so you can see it. I'll give you a key and you can settle in there. Bring your things up. Once that is done, take the rest of the morning and get to Mandy's store and buy what you need. Grab yourself some lunch and some groceries, and I am expecting you back here at two o'clock this afternoon. You are going to have a late night, and tomorrow, on Saturdays, we work a half day. And when you are out shopping, get some soap and towels. You smell, Thomas."

I did smell. But it was the last time.

***

The next six weeks were glorious. At least to me. I was working and earning money. I had a place to live although it was small, and I had a bed and regular food. Mr. Turner was a decent man, and we got along. The furniture making was going well, and I asked if I could take leftover woods and carve and whittle at night, which I did. My three books were placed on the small desk up in my apartment, and I had new (to me) clothes and socks and boots that fit. Before the winter set in, I went back to Mandy's second-hand store and purchased a heavy coat and some gloves whose very small holes I was able to repair. I thought things could not get better. I was happier than I remembered being for years.

And in all this change, in all this happiness, something even better occurred. Something that would change my life. I met an angel. I met Mr. Turner's sixteen-year-old daughter, Ava Turner, and for the first time, I fell in love.

Chapter 4   1915

It was the last day of sixth grade, and Tomas woke early to complete his chores before getting to the schoolhouse ahead of the other students. This was the day of the school picnic when a baseball game was planned, lunches would be shared outside, and because some of the mothers had volunteered their skills at baking, sweets in the form of cookies and cakes would be available. Awards would also be given for various achievements, and Tomas was aware that he would be receiving at least two of them: the reading and the ciphering awards. He knew that he was in the running for the "Student of the Year" award which came with the enormous prize of two dollars. But the reason Tomas wanted to get to school so early was to speak with the teacher, Mr. Everett Jensen, and explain to him that he would not be returning to complete all eight years of schooling.

Everett Jensen had taken over teaching duties for the Levett School when Tomas started second grade. Mr. Jensen's two-year teaching certificate from the Illinois State Normal University had prepared him to teach all the grades at the school, but he also had some innovative ideas of his own. His first year of teaching was difficult because the students were used to the fun, flexible, and fluid teaching style of Miss Schaller who left to get married. Mr. Jensen believed in a rigorous curriculum. He taught using both the traditional approaches of rote and memorization, and the progressive innovations of scientific methodology, individual needs, and societal requirements. At first the students were bewildered and shocked, but soon they accepted, then appreciated the lessons. At least the younger ones seemed to. Some of the older students, particularly the boys, decided that another year or two of the sorts of activities and work required by this teacher was not worth the certificate garnered at the eighth year's end, so they halted their education. Those who remained flourished, and Tomas Allerton flourished most of all.

It was not that Tomas had no friends at the school, but his leisure time was spoken for, and he didn't join the other boys in games, or fishing expeditions, or hiking in the forest, and sleeping outside in the woods when the weather permitted. He got along with the students, playing at recess and lunchtime, but after the school day, he was expected to come straight home. His father had made this perfectly clear to Tomas. He woke up early to complete chores around the farm before walking the half mile to school, and he was to come directly home to complete additional tasks and duties. Some days Tomas was kept home from school to help his father with special carpentry projects, or deliveries of the completed undertakings, or, rarely, the funeral services for which the father, because he made caskets, was asked to facilitate.

As he aged, Tomas began working in the woodshop as apprentice to his father. Between the farm duties and the woodshop responsibilities, there was little time for playing. As Tomas grew and excelled in school, he cherished what extra time was his to read the books Mr. Jensen loaned him. School, as it turned out, was the easiest enterprise undertaken by him, and the one his father resented the most. So, when Tomas was twelve, almost thirteen, his father decreed those six years of schooling were sufficient. After all, working on the farm and as a carpenter did not necessitate an eighth-grade certificate.

On the last day of his formal education, Tomas arrived at the school building and was relieved to find Mr. Jensen inside and the door propped open. He walked up the stairs and knocked, and Mr. Jensen looked up from his daily task of cleaning the desks and smiled. Tomas entered and placed the most recently loaned book on the teacher's desk.

"Tomas, come in. You're early, but I'm glad you're here. It will give us a few minutes to discuss *The Call of the Wild*. What did you think of it? Tell me as I finish this," and Me. Jensen gave the last desk a wipe as he stood up.

"Mr. Jensen, the book was great, and I was surprised by the dog being the main character, but that's not why I'm here early."

Mr. Jensen put his cleaning tools away and turned to look at Tomas. He appreciated this youngster. Tomas had challenged him as a teacher, and he was grateful for it. The academic ability and natural mental alacrity of the boy allowed him to advance rapidly, and Mr. Jensen was pleased at his progress. He knew that Tomas deserved the Student of the Year award he would receive later in the day. The challenge of the last few years was to keep Tomas engaged and active, and the teacher looked forward to the next couple of years teaching and guiding him. In fact, he was thinking about how to get Tomas into a high school. There were some high schools in the city of Champaign, but Tomas would need to live there, and that presented a problem. Mr. Jensen knew some people in that city and might be able to arrange for Tomas to stay with someone, but he wasn't sure how the boy's father would take to his son leaving the farm. These were issues to be worked out.

"What is it, Tomas?"

"Sir, I won't be returning to school in the fall, and I just wanted to tell you that I appreciate all the things you've done for me. I learned a lot, and I want you to know that."

Mr. Jensen looked closely at the boy. Tomas had grown in the past year and was tall for his age. But despite his nearly six feet of height, he looked ready to cry. Mr. Jensen sat down at his desk and motioned for Tomas to take a seat.

"What has happened, Tomas? Why won't you be back?"

Tomas took a deep breath. "My father said I have had enough schooling and don't need any more. I am to work with him as a full-time apprentice in his woodshop, and on the farm. He said that I don't need a certificate to do what he does, so this is my last year."

Mr. Jensen was silent for a bit as his considered what to say. He had met the boy's father briefly a few times, although he never came to any of the end-of-year programs like the other fathers had. Most of the men were proud of their children's accomplishments, but Tomas' father didn't appear to be interested. He looked at Tomas whose head was lowered.

"Tomas, after school today, I will go and speak with your father. I can explain to him how academically gifted you are and how you could earn a high school diploma. I didn't intend to say anything to you yet and was going to wait until next term, but I think I have an idea about that."

Tomas looked up and shook his head violently. "NO! Sorry, Mr. Jensen, but my father won't allow that. He's set in his ways, and I don't think he'll listen at all. I can't think that he would ever allow me to leave the farm to go to a high school."

"I can talk to him, Tomas. I am sure he will listen. What parent doesn't want their child to achieve an education? You have done so well and are far beyond any of the other students, and I wouldn't just say this. I mean it. Your grades are the highest and so are your scores. You read at the same level I do, and our conversations about books show me that you are a careful and thoughtful reader and thinker. Let me go and explain this to your father."

"Please, Mr. Jensen, I know him. He won't listen. Please."

The teacher looked at Tomas. The boy seemed panicked, and perhaps he was right. He considered what to do.

"Well, let's do this. I won't come and speak to your father right away. I'll wait until closer to the fall term, and then I will visit. But we can continue the reading and discussion we have started. I brought another book for you, and perhaps in a few weeks, we can meet to talk about it. Maybe then your father will be more willing to speak to me. Is that acceptable to you?"

Tomas looked at his teacher. "I don't think he will change his mind, but I would appreciate any books you have to loan me, and I will be pleased to read them. I'm not sure when I could meet and talk to you about them. My father keeps me pretty busy, and we have plenty of orders we need to fill this summer. We will probably be working from sun to sun on them. At least that's what he said."

Mr. Jensen looked at the beautifully crafted wooden paper weight Tomas had given to him last Christmas. The boy had made it, and it was as fine a carving as Mr. Jensen had ever seen. Obviously, the boy had talents that went beyond academics.

"Do you like working with the wood, Tomas?"

Tomas smiled. "I do. I'm good at it too, at least that is what my father said once, and he isn't given to compliments. I just took to it, and it comes naturally to me. Sort of like the reading did."

"I can see that. You have talents, Tomas, and need to cherish them. Did you ever hear that, 'It is not in our stars to hold our destiny, but in ourselves'?"

"No, Sir. Who said that, and what does it mean?"

"That's from the next reading I am giving you," and the teacher reached into the middle drawer of his desk and pulled out a slim volume.

"Here, Tomas, this is your next reading. You haven't read any Shakespeare yet that I know of, so this will be a challenge for you. It's a play called *Julius Caesar*."

"Is that the man you told us about? The *Ides of March* story you told the class?"

"That's him. I'm not pretending this will be easy reading, but I believe you will be able to get something out of it, and we can talk about your observations when we meet."

Tomas went to the desk and took the volume and glanced through it. "That's a problem. If I'm not coming to school anymore, I don't think we can meet. Maybe I shouldn't take this book."

"Let's do this. You're still going to church on Sunday, right?"

"Yes. My father doesn't go and doesn't really like me going, but I do. I need to get away from the farm sometimes."

"If you can come a bit earlier, we could speak before church, and I will walk part way home with you afterwards. We can talk about the reading then, even if it's a brief discussion. Does that sound like it will work?"

Tomas smiled. "I think so," and they both glanced out the door because they heard the noise of additional students coming towards the schoolhouse.

"Great. Then in two weeks from this Sunday, let's plan on meeting twenty minutes before the service begins. Can you do that?"

"Yes, Sir. I can and will. Thank you again, Mr. Jensen. I really appreciate all you have done for me."

The man stood up and held out his hand to the boy who shook it. Both felt that the future was bound to be a bright one; that somehow, the boy's father would be made to understand how important education was; that Tomas would be able to finish his two years and receive his certificate; that a high school diploma was within the boy's grasp; that Tomas's destiny would include more than just farm work. They both felt hopeful and optimistic. They would both be disappointed.

Chapter 5   1919 – 1921

I met her in winter.

It was the Christmas season, and while there wasn't much snow on the ground, it was cold, and a gusty wind blew around me whenever I walked outside. I was grateful for the heavy coat and winter gloves and hat I had purchased from Hank, the manager of Mandy's Second-Hand Store. Mr. Turner continued to be kind to me, and I considered how different life might have been if he, or someone like him, had been my father. We continued working side by side, and while he was usually quiet, he spoke about his family. He had two children. He and his wife and daughter lived just on the outskirts of the main town, about a mile or so from the shop, and he drove his automobile to work every day. His daughter, Ava was sixteen and his son, Aaron, was twenty and married, so he didn't live with them but stayed in Michigan on a small farm. Mrs. Turner gave piano lessons, and Ava was an expert musician. They lived in a large house and Mr. Turner had made all the furniture for it. I learned all these facts while working alongside him. His family sounded like a perfect family, and I envied their life.

On Tuesday, December 24, we worked only half a day. Mr. Turner closed shop early, and we would not work the next day. It was Christmas. The holiday had never meant much to me, and my father refused to celebrate it except for the few times we had driven to Champaign to have dinner with Aunt Jennifer's family. But there were decorations in the windows of the town stores, and people would say, "Merry Christmas!" to strangers they passed on the streets. All of this was new to me, and it made me think about what I missed in the years on the farm. Before he left on that Tuesday, Mr. Turner invited me to Christmas dinner at their house.

"Dinner will be at one in the afternoon, and if you don't mind a walk in the cold, you are welcomed to be with us. I know you have no family, and it's a shame for someone to be alone on this day. My family is anxious to meet you. I've told them what a good carpenter and worker you are and how you have helped this business. Our neighbors will also come, and we should be a merry group. What do you think?"

I thought it was wonderful, and I told him so. He gave me instructions for getting to his house and said that if I left at noon, that should be plenty to time to walk there. Before he left, he turned to me and said, "By the way, Thomas, I thought that an appropriate Christmas gift for you would be money, and I hope you will accept it. I will not require you to pay rent for the next two weeks, so your full pay of ten dollars will be given. Merry Christmas, and I'll see you tomorrow,"

I wished him a *Merry Christmas* also, the first time those words had left my mouth in years, and as soon as he left, I hurried over to Mandy's store, hoping it was still open. It was, and with the help of Hank, I found a used suit and dress shirt and tie to wear the next day. It was my first suit, and I was delighted with it. Back at the apartment, I tried it all on again, prancing in front of the small mirror above the dresser, looking at myself and realizing I had no idea how to use the necktie and wondered why I didn't ask. However, even without it, I looked splendid, although it was uncomfortably tight. I bathed carefully that night, washed my hair thoroughly, and cleaned my nails the best I could. I was ready.

It was cold, but not snowy, and once dressed, I started out on my journey. It was strange walking through the almost deserted town, but soon I could see the Turner house, and I looked forward to its warmth. The three-story house loomed before me, and as I walked up its stairs and let the door knocker fall three times, I was as excited as I had ever been. Mr. Turner answered the door and had me stand in the hallway. He spoke to me as I removed my coat and gloves and hat, and stomped my boots, trying to rid them of the snow.

"Here, let me show you to the downstairs bathroom so you can wash up. When you are done, come into the front parlor and meet everyone. We are just getting ready to toast the holiday," and he led me to the room which was practically as large as my apartment.

After I felt readied, I followed the sound of talking and laughter to the front parlor which was decorated with the largest Christmas tree I had even seen, not that I'd seen that many. I was introduced to Mrs. Turner and the neighbors, the Wilsons and their two young sons. Mrs. Turner handed me a fancy glass cup which contained a frothy liquid and said, "Just as soon as Ava gets here, we will toast the season, and then we will go into the dining room. We are glad you have joined us, Mr. Allerton."

I smiled and held the glass cup which contained something called *eggnog*, and I was careful not to spill it. I brought it to my lips to take a small sip of the fullness just as Mr. Turner said, "Here she is. Come, Ava, we are waiting for you." I turned to see his daughter.

I choked on the sip and coughed. I could not take my eyes from the most beautiful girl I had ever seen. Ava was slight, just five feet tall, but she was perfect in every respect. Her hair was the color of white-gold, and it was piled on her head, and some sort of sparkly decoration surrounded her forehead and curved up onto her hair. Her eyes were so large I wondered that they could fit in her lovely face, and I could see their blueness from across the room. She didn't walk but seemed to float, and as I was introduced to her, she gave me the loveliest of smiles and welcomed me. I blushed and felt a heat creeping up my face. Her mother handed her a cup, and everyone turned to Mr. Turner who held his up, said some appropriate words, and we toasted the holiday before entering the dining room where I was seated across from Ava. The dining room was astounding in its spaciousness, and the food was amazing and delicious, but I could not take my eyes from Ava's face.

After dinner, we went to what was called the *music room*, and listened to Ava and her mother take turns playing the piano and singing Christmas songs. Mrs. Turner encouraged us all to join in, and I felt stupid because I did not know the words. Ava noticed I wasn't singing, so as her mother continued to play, she brought a songbook to me.

"Mr. Allerton, if you don't mind sharing this, we can sing together. Here are the words," and as she smiled, I felt my heart melt into a pool. I was never a singer, but I believe that was my most enthusiastic performance. We shared the book, and I was completely disappointed when the singing ended. I would have been happy for it to continue until the next Christmas.

I didn't feel the cold as I walked back to my apartment. I thought only about the white-gold softness which brushed against my hand as we bent to pick up the dropped book, the sea-blueness of those eyes, and the velvet smoothness of her hand as she shook mine good-night and said, "I'm glad to have met you." The snow fell into my face, and it felt calming and comforting and cheering.

*****

I married her in spring.

Once Mr. Turner accepted that I knew what I was doing, that I could be trusted and was dependable, he raised my salary to twelve dollars a week. Of course, I only received ten of that with the other two paying my rent. I became a regular guest at the Turner house for Sunday dinners and family occasions. I was sure part of that was due to Mr. Turner's concern about my having no family and being alone. But most of it, as Ava later told me, was due to her insistence that I be invited.

Ava's seventeenth birthday was in late February. I worked nightly on a special gift for her. It was a keepsake box which I carved in a most intricate manner. Inside the box was placed a small chiseled bird, whose wings were out-stretched in flight. It took many long hours to get it just right, and I was anxious to give it to her. There was a dinner for her birthday. I was invited, and walked through an awful snowstorm to get there, but I didn't care. I was anxious to see her. Neighbors of the Turners and friends of Ava were invited also, but I hoped to find some time alone with her to give her the gift.

When I was able to catch her alone, I wasn't sure what to say, so I just handed her the box. I had nothing to wrap it in, and said simply, "Here, Ava, I made this for you. Happy birthday." She examined the box and when she opened it and saw the bird, she laughed and said, "What a wonder, Thomas! This is lovely. You are so inventive." She reached up and kissed my cheek, and I determined then to marry her.

Of course, I was only sixteen, but everyone thought I was eighteen. I wasn't sure how a marriage worked or how one went about it, but I was determined to find out. I couldn't ask Mr. Turner, and I was busy at the shop, so I had no friends, but I thought that Hank from Mandy's Second-Hand Store could help. The following week, during a lunch break, I asked Mr. Turner if I could have the time to pick up some needed items at Mandy's, and left for the store.

Hank was straightening out the shoes. When I walked in, he called, "Well, Tommy. Good to see you. What can I help you get today? Look, there are some barely used boots here, and I think these will fit you."

I walked over to look at the boots I did not want. I picked them up and turned them around and looked at this man who was the closest I had to a friend. "Hank, how does someone go about getting married? What is the process?"

Hank looked at me. "Well, only here for a few months, and you already have a sweetheart? Fast work, Tommy. Anyone I know?"

I explained to him about Ava. I asked what I should do, and he listened carefully to me before he answered.

"Tommy, I think you need to give this some time. You have only seen her, what…five times? Six times? Does she already have a beau? How will you support the two of you? Where will you live? Have you talked to her father yet? That is something you need to consider. You are still young…eighteen, right? Why rush?"

I listened, and we spoke more, and he gave me advice and told me how marriages worked, and then, I needed to get back to the shop. I thanked him, and asked if we could talk another time. I needed to consider what he said. Before I left, I tried on the boots which fit. I bought them as a thank-you.

As winter faded away, I began to see Ava more often. She would come into town, driving the horse and wagon, to go shopping with her mother. She would stop in the shop to greet her father. And me. I began to go to Sunday service at the Methodist Church because I knew the Turners went there, and when the weather cleared and the roads weren't so muddy, Ava and I would walk back to her house after the church service where I would have Sunday dinner with them. Mr. Turner seemed pleased I was there, but I began to suspect that Mrs. Turner wasn't too happy about things. Ava was thin and slight and given to catching colds, and Mrs. Turner thought that the exercise and weather was unhealthy for her, but we continued our walking.

Ava and I were keeping company. That's what Hank said we were doing. I had become friends with Hank, who was married and older than me by ten years. He was really older by twelve years, but he didn't know that. His wife was going to have a child, and Hank seemed to know all the answers to the questions I had. When Ava and I did marry, Hank and his wife were the only guests I invited to the wedding luncheon.

At the end of a rainy April, as Ava and I were sitting on her porch one Sunday, waiting for the rain to stop so I could walk home, I knew the time had come. There was a silence between us, and I got up my nerve and took her hand and told her she was the only woman I ever wanted to marry, and would she? She would, but I had to talk to her father first. My heart sank, and I swallowed hard.

"I will, but I can't today. I need to go home and think about my speech. Tomorrow at work I'll approach him. Do you think there is anything important I need to say to him?"

Ava looked at me and shrugged. "My parents, especially my mother, have always worried about my health. I was never very hearty when young, and maybe if you tell Father that you will care for me and my health and that he shouldn't worry, it might make a difference. Whatever you say to him he will tell Mother, so keep that in mind."

I nodded. The rain had stopped and it was time for me to leave. I pressed Ava's hand, brought it to my lips, and kissed it. She turned to see if her parents were watching and then kissed my cheek. I jumped joyously off the stairs and made her laugh as I raced to the end of her street. When I got there, I turned and saw her standing on the porch looking at me, and I waved for at least a minute before walking back.

Mr. Turner listened to my prepared speech the following day and said he would discuss the matter with his wife. There were many discussions, and I was asked many questions, and finally, after I had made numerous promises and agreed to their demands, Ava and I were given permission to marry. One Friday morning, at the end of May, wearing my almost new suit and a necktie tied correctly, in front of the minister of the Newtown Methodist Church and a small gathering of friends and neighbors, Ava and I were married. At the luncheon afterwards, my friend Hank came up to congratulate me and wish me luck. Because his wife had just given birth a few days ago, she was unable to attend, but my wife (it sounded so strange to say that) made sure Hank had a piece of the wedding cake to take home to her.

That afternoon, after the luncheon was over and the guests were gone, Ava and I drove the Turner's horse and buggy to my apartment. I had cleaned it up and organized my clothes and belongings, and packed my knapsack and folded the bedroll. I gathered everything up, placed it in the back of the wagon, and with my new bride, drove back through the town to the large Turner house. We were going to live there with her parents, and the third-floor bedroom, the one farthest away from the one her parents had on the opposite end of the second floor, was where we spent our wedding night and made our home. When we went to our room that night, Ava placed the keepsake box with the carved bird in it on top of our dresser, and we smiled at each other.

***

I buried her in summer.

We were happy. I don't think either of us knew what to expect in a marriage, and despite the advice Hank gave me, nothing compared to the two of us learning together. There were mornings I was embarrassed to leave our bedroom and greet the Turners downstairs for breakfast. And the first weeks, as Mr. Turner drove his automobile into town and I sat beside him, I believe I maintained a permanent blush on my face. I was determined to get over it and to show that I was an adult, so I worked harder and faster and longer at the shop. I wanted to thank Mr. Turner for being my father-in-law and make my my wife proud of me. My mother-in-law was another matter. She was unhappy that I had married Ava, and as I came down for breakfast, often with Ava on my arm and the two of us laughing, I would be given side looks which told me exactly what she thought about me and about what I was doing with her daughter. Nothing was ever said, but I knew.

In September of 1920, Ava gave me a birthday dinner to celebrate my nineteenth birthday, although I knew I was just seventeen. She had made a special cake for me, and afterwards, she played the piano while I sat next to her on the bench. We each had another piece of the cake before going to our room, and I don't think I ever had a better birthday. Since there were no celebrations when I was young, except for the few times Aunt Jennifer treated me, this was a special time.

That fall continued to be filled with new experiences and celebrations of holidays I never knew about. There was a pumpkin-parade held in town at the end of October, and Ava and I went to see the town's children dressed in costumes, marching down the street. Then the Thanksgiving Day feast was spectacular, and Ava's brother, Aaron and his wife, Reba came in for a week's visit. I got along with him and wished he didn't live so far away. I would have liked to claim him as a friend.

Christmas was special. Because I was earning a salary and saving much of it, I was able to buy presents for my new family. Mr. Turner received a new tie, and I bought a lovely shawl that Ava had noticed in one of the town store windows. Even the embroidered handkerchiefs I gave to Mrs. Turner got a smile from her, and while I cherished the winter scarf Ava had knitted for me, it was the gift she gave me on Christmas night that was exceptional.

We had wished the neighbors and friends who had come for dinner a *Merry Christmas* and everyone left. Ava hadn't felt well for a few weeks, and I was worried when she ate almost nothing at dinner, and excused herself twice during it. Once we were in our bedroom, I asked if she were well.

"Thomas, I am fine. Perhaps better than I have ever been, and I have another gift for you."

I looked around for a wrapped present, but she smiled and came close to me. "Here it is," and she took my hand and placed it against her stomach. "This is your gift, although it will be a few months until you will be allowed to hold it."

I had no idea what she was talking about. Sometimes my stupidity got in the way. I looked at her, saw her long white-gold hair drifting down her back and thought she was enough of a gift, and I told her that.

She laughed. "No, Thomas, next summer you will have something else. A daughter or son. I'm going to have a baby. That's why I haven't felt good and had to leave the table so often. You are going to be a father!"

To say I was shocked doesn't even closely describe my feelings. I was stunned, dumbfounded, thunderstruck. I was petrified and startled and panicked. I sat down on the edge of the bed and could not speak. To be sure, this wasn't the response I realize I should have given Ava, but I had no other. She took my nervousness for joy, and when she hugged me, I put my arms around her and held on. She may have been pregnant, but I felt I was going to be sick.

I got used to the idea and began to welcome it. I didn't know how to be a father, and had only a bad example to guide me. But I thought that if I could take Mr. Turner's model and use it as a blueprint, I would do well. That was my plan. I worried about Ava constantly because her frailness became more pronounced. The doctor made many visits, and Mrs. Turner fussed and worried all the time. I did what I could to entertain Ava, but I noted that except for her growing front, she seemed haggard and thin and always seemed to be tired. Because the flights of stairs became too much for her to handle, Mr. Turner and I spent the better part of an early summer week reorganizing the library at the back of the first floor into a bedroom for Ava. I was expected to leave her rest at night and climb the stairs to be in our bedroom by myself. I did that because I was instructed to by Mrs. Turner, and I wanted no arguments to upset Ava. Each night, I tucked her in and talked with her and kissed her good-night, and then I trucked up the stairs to go to bed. Alone.

The summer heat was brutal for all of us, especially Ava. Mr. Turner special-ordered three Westinghouse pedestal electric fans to make everyone, especially Ava more comfortable. However, the noise bothered her, and she grew chilled, so the fan was removed from her room and taken to the shop where it succeeded in blowing around the bits of wood and stirred up the dust. I no longer worked late at night, but came home to check on Ava and spend as much time with her as I could.

One July night, as I sat on the side of her bed, holding cool cloths to her sweaty face, she talked about names for the baby. Her voice had changed, becoming softer and somewhat raspy, and I leaned down to hear her.

"Thomas, let's call a daughter Elizabeth Ava, and if it's a son, I would like to name him after Father. *James* should be his first name. But his middle name should be *Thomas*. What do you think?"

I took another cloth and squeezed the wetness from it and placed it on her forehead. "I think that's perfect. And whichever we get this time, I'm sure we'll have the opposite the next time and will be able to use both names," and I leaned down to kiss her cheek. She smiled weakly at me and then shuddered and moaned which panicked me. "What's wrong? Are you sick? Should I get your mother?"

Ava took a deep breath and closed her eyes. She sighed and said, "Just a pain. They have been coming on and off all day. It's a few weeks early for the baby, so I don't think that's it. Just the heat I suppose," and as I brushed her hair which had grown wet from the cloths on her face, she drifted off to sleep. I waited for another quarter of an hour, and then, as her breathing settled, I left for my room.

She had been ill in the night, and had finally fallen asleep. Mrs. Turner was sitting in her room, watching her, when Mr. Turner and I left for the shop. We were working, finishing up a table and chairs which had been ordered. In the late afternoon, Mr. Castle from two stores down knocked loudly on the front door and then came in without waiting. Mr. Turner's workshop had no telephone, but Mr. Castle's shop did, and he entered to let us know that the doctor telephoned with a message for us. He had been called to the house after we left, and now he wanted us both to come home. Quickly.

We closed the shop, got in the automobile, and Mr. Turner, who was always careful and slow, drove the fastest I had ever witnessed him drive. When we arrived at the house, we both jumped out of the car which was parked behind the doctor's and ran into the house. There was noise and weeping going on in Ava's downstairs bedroom, and we both hurried to the door. The housekeeper and Mrs. Turner were there, and the doctor was wrapping a blanket around a small object. When he saw us, he shook his head, and I ran to Ava's side where the coldness had not yet set in. I took her limp hand, and called her name, and I must have become wild, because soon Mr. Turner had his arm around me, and he and the doctor sat me in a chair, and I put my head in my hands. The doctor took the small dead child and placed him in my arms, and that was the only time I held my son, James Thomas.

***

I left in the fall.

Ava and James Thomas were buried together. The shawl I had given her for Christmas was arranged around her thin shoulders, and her arms were wrapped around our son. Somehow, I got through the rest of the summer, not caring that between the July and August heat and my disinterest in eating, weight was dropping from my frame. Mrs. Turner remained in her bedroom and was rarely seen. The housekeeper brought a full tray up to her room three times a day, and then, three times a day, brought the full tray down. Mr. Turner, a naturally quiet man, turned totally silent, and the house the three of us occupied became a mausoleum for the living. If that was living. When Mr. Turner came to me on a Sunday evening at the start of September with a dictate from Mrs. Turner, I was not surprised. She wanted me out of the house. She blamed me for Ava's death. She had no daughter, no grandson, and it was my fault. She could no longer bear my presence. I understood.

I walked up the stairs to the bedroom Ava and I had shared and packed my belongings. I looked at the keepsake box containing the carved bird and placed it in the knapsack. I rolled up a bedroll and holding whatever I could carry, walked back to the apartment above the woodshop. Using the key Mr. Turner had given me, I went in. I set everything on the small desk and thin table, and walked down the stairs to the shop. To keep busy, I completed a chair. When I finished, I walked up the stairs to the apartment, made some tea, and fell into a mournful sleep.

Monday morning, I woke up and went to work. I began another project that had been ordered, but Mr. Turner never came in. Again, I worked until late and then went to bed. The next day, I was in the shop and Mr. Turner pushed open the door and entered. He set down the lunch the housekeeper had made, put his carpenter's apron on, and we worked together on the projects. We didn't speak except for what was necessary. That continued the remainder of Tuesday and Wednesday and Thursday morning.

On Thursday afternoon, he stopping working early to go home to his heartbroken wife and empty house. At the front door, he turned to me and said, "I'm sorry, Thomas." I nodded my head in acknowledgement of whatever the apology was meant for, and he left. I finished cleaning the shop, sweeping, putting tools back, drawing the shades, turning out the lights, and then went up the back stairs.

It was five o'clock, and I sat in the dark apartment thinking. After an hour, I got up and packed. I took my knapsack and organized it. The bedroll secured my three books and carving tools. I left my suit, the one I was married in, hanging on a hook, and took only what I knew I would need. I lifted everything onto my back, locked the door, and went down the rickety stairs one last time. I opened the shop door and walked through to Mr. Turner's office. Before I left for the final time, on his desk in the office, I placed the key to the shop, the key for the apartment, and in the middle of the desk, where Mr. Turner would see it the following day, a keepsake box which I had carved in a most intricate manner. Inside the box was placed a small chiseled bird whose wings were out-stretched in flight.

Chapter 6   1912

The first time Tomas helped his father lift a body into the casket he had helped to build, he was nine years old. The body was that of old Mrs. Henderson. The Hendersons were one of the founding families of the town, and they had the second largest family gravesite in the area. A century of Hendersons was buried in the ground out to the south of their farm where the stones were surrounded by a grave fence to keep the spirits of the dead from interfering with the living. For as long as could be remembered, the family had relied on past generations of the Allertons for the eternity boxes needed. There were a few families in the rural area surrounding the town of Levett, just north of Champaign in Champaign County, Illinois, who still stuck with the old ways of honoring their dead. Most of the townspeople used the services of the Richards Funeral Parlor found in the next town, but the older families still relied on the services of the Allerton carpenters and furniture makers, Tomas' father being of that line.

The father did not make many caskets any more, but when he had time and nothing else to create, he would have Tomas help him gather the wood, measure, cut, hand drill the holes for the thick rope handles, join the floor, the sides, ready the lid. Additional trim was done as requested by various families, although the Hendersons were simple people and for them, plain pine, no staining of the wood or fanciness of the trim was necessary. Unworldliness when meeting the Maker was what the Henderson family wanted. Tomas' father put his son to work. *The practice is good for the boy*, he thought. *After all, I helped my grandfather at his age.*

Tomas enjoyed the work and didn't think about what would be placed into the large boxes they created. But when his father was asked to serve as undertaker for Alma Henderson, Tomas was told that he would assist. He was not expecting to lift the shrouded body of the old woman into the box. The father prepared him as they drove the horse and wagon loaded with the casket to the Hendersons. Because it was so rare for his father to talk to him, he listened intently and even asked a few questions.

"I have to touch the body?"

His father nodded. "It's not a terrible thing to do. It won't take long, and then I'll ask some of the men to help carry it into their parlor. That's really all we'll need to do. Except, after the casket is placed on the table, and everything is arranged as the family wants it, we should stand in front of it, bow our heads, and pretend to say a prayer."

"Pretend or really pray?"

The father sighed. He wanted to tell his son that it didn't matter one way or the other, but he just shrugged and said, "Just bow your head and keep your eyes on the floor. When you hear me whisper 'Amen', you can look up. It's just what's expected. Then I'll say something to the sons, get paid, and we'll leave. Won't take that long. Nothing to be worried about."

Tomas felt a quivering in his stomach. It was one thing to visit his mother and brothers and family members at his own family gravesite, but he hadn't seen a dead body before. Well, there was his grandmother, but he had been four and didn't remember much about it. He knew by now, having lived with his father for the past three years, that he just needed to do what he was told. It had been a while since he had received one of those thumps on his head for refusing a task, and he didn't want to acquire another. He only wished he hadn't been taken out of school to help with this charge. But it was Friday, and he would return on Monday, and he knew better than to complain. Or even mention it.

They pulled up to the Henderson house, and the father got out to speak to the man standing on the front porch who directed him to the back. The horse pulled the wagon to its destination, and after stopping the father climbed down and motioned for Tomas to come and stand beside him. Three men came out to the back and helped the father move the casket to the back bedroom where Alma Henderson had been positioned. She was clothed in a shroud and ready for placement. Some women from the family who were standing by the bed carefully placed a special blanket and pillow into the box, and once they left, his father looked at Tomas.

"Mrs. Henderson wasn't a fleshy woman, and she don't weigh much. I'll get her under the shoulders, and you lift her feet up. Just be careful as we place her down."

Tomas did as instructed. He held his breath and lifted the shrouded feet, feeling the soft slippers underneath the gauzy material. He tried not to look down, but watched his father who had most of the weight, and once Mrs. Henderson was placed snugly into her resting place, Tomas stepped back and breathed out. The father looked at him and nodded, and then went out to ask some of the men to help carry the box, in sober procession, to the parlor where the dining room table had been moved and readied. Once the box was in place, two of the women unfolded a solemn black and brown decorated quilt, and placed it on top of the casket to comfort the woman inside who would never be warm again. Everyone stood back and his father motioned to Tomas to stand next to him where they bowed their heads and contrived a prayer-like attitude. When he heard the 'Amen" whispered *sotto voice*, Tomas looked up at his father.

They were done. His father spoke to the people standing around, silent and intense, gave his condolences, and then the man who had been on the front porch, walked with them to the back door. Tomas was sent out to stand by the wagon as the shaking of hands and exchange of payment took place. Then the man went inside, closing the door behind him, and the father turned to look at Tomas.

Without knowing it would happen, and not expecting it to, Tomas suddenly bent over and rid himself of his morning breakfast onto the gravel beside the wagon. Twice. He stood up, took a deep breath, wiped his mouth with his sleeve, and looked over at his father expecting a scolding. His father looked at him, and sighed. "First time I helped my grandfather, I did the same thing. Come on, boy. Get in the wagon. Fresh air will help."

They climbed into the wagon and the father took the reins. He clicked his tongue, said "Git, now" to the horse, and they traveled back to the farm where for the balance of the day, Tomas was allowed his freedom.

***

For the remainder of the years Tomas and his father lived together, there were only a handful of additional times they were required to act as undertakers. Tomas dreaded these instances, but knew he couldn't refuse the tasks. He understood his duties at the farm and the woodshop, and his father made it very clear to him that refusal to do anything would result in physical harshness. Something to be avoided.

The relationship between father and son was not an easy one. Tomas remembered living with his Aunt Jennifer and Uncle David after his mother's death, and he missed them after they moved to the city of Champaign. On the rare occasions he saw them, his aunt would hug him and kiss his cheek and inquire about his schooling and activities and ask if he were happy. He always answered *yes* to the last question. He knew better than to deny happiness. He had once, in the early years, and when they returned to the farm, his father made it clear that Tomas *was* happy, and the next time he was asked, would admit so.

Not that the father mistreated him often, other than necessary head thumps, but he needed to instill in him responsibility, productivity, and obedience, traits he believed were essential. Without Tomas' mother around, little affection was rendered to him except from Molly the dog (actually a series of dogs named *Molly*). Food, shelter, and clothing were provided. Other than Aunt Jennifer's birthday treats (a cake or cookies, and a dollar slipped into Tomas' pocket), that day was ignored. Christmas was the only time dinner was shared with Aunt Jennifer, Uncle David, and whatever additional relatives showed up. Tomas looked forward to that celebration because the dinner leftovers were sent back with them, and they fed Tomas and his father for a couple days, a delicious remembrance of the holiday when another dollar was slipped to Tomas. As long as he completed his chores, and helped in the woodshop, and didn't get in trouble in school, life at the farm was stable.

Tomas' father wasn't naturally unkind. Ill-naturedness had developed slowly. Life, especially since the death of his wife, had been grim. He struggled by himself on the farm, attempting to care for the small vegetable garden, keep the few animals around alive, work in the the woodshop creating furniture and other items to sell so that he would have some ready cash. There was guilt because he couldn't nurture or watch a young child, and when Jennifer offered to keep Tomas with her family after the death of her sister, he felt he had no choice. He wanted to keep this son alive. There were three dead children buried next to his wife, and he was terrified of there being a fourth. The lonely years crafted a man who was brooding and taciturn and despondent. He did not understand how to raise a child with affection. Too much fondness or tenderness or care, and fate would take this one, this last one, away, so he kept his approach to the boy detached. Should this one be lost, at least his heart would be preserved. Impassivity was the best course.

He gave Tomas something more beneficial than affection. He gave him the knowledge he had. He tutored him, shared his expertise, imparted the understanding he had about wood. He taught his only living son what his grandfather had communicated to him: the trees that were available in the surrounding woodlands for their use: how to fell them, remove the branches, cut the trunk, peel the bark, season the timbers. And when there was not the type of wood or the size needed, he explained where the closest sawmills were, and when they traveled to them, Tomas learned how to get the best price, the fairest exchange. When they returned, they stacked the wood correctly and safely, and when it was needed, he taught the boy how to choose which of the woods should be used for the project, and how to consider the grain, the changes in moisture, differences and varieties in sawn boards, the complexities of joinery, the uses of hardening oil, varnishes, and wax blends. Tool usage, safety considerations, cleaning obligations, all these things were given to Tomas in the place of warmth and attachment. The work brought comfort to the boy, and the sparse amiability which fogged the woodshop mitigated acrimony. Most of the time.

Over the years, Tomas became an expert, supplanting his father who struggled with both his own pride and his own humility. In the coldness of the winter, when days were too icy to continue formal schooling or stay in the woodshop to complete projects, Tomas first watched and then practiced wood carving and whittling. Small objects: canes, keepsake boxes, carved animal toys, pinwheel whirligigs, were created in the warmth of the house, next to the stove. When completed, they were stacked away until spring when they would be taken to the town's general store and offered for sale. The carving and whittling passed the time, and the handiwork brought in extra cash, and as with the larger items: the fence posts, the bed frames, blanket chests, window and door casings, baseboards and moldings, caskets, Tomas seemed to have a knack for both whittling and carving.

He, again, surpassed his father who watched as his son took a piece of green wood or pine, and using the sharp carving knife and the gouge and chisel, make a sheep whose lumbered wool looked ready to shear while it was almost possible to hear its chiseled mouth bleat. The shaped horse's tail looked coarse to the touch, the mane seemed as silk, and the upper lip of the animal looked as if it were ready to grasp the grass and deliver it to the teeth to be chewed. The staff of the cane Tomas whittled was topped with the face and beard of an old man whose cheeks were wrinkled, eyes were slightly crossed, and the nose had just a tad of a bump to it, looking very similar, too much so, to Mr. Nelson, the owner of the general store. And the more he worked at the cedar keepsake boxes, the whimsey chains, the carved heart-shaped paper weights from the oak which was so hard to work that the father never tried, the more skilled Tomas became. And without acknowledging it to himself, a resentfulness built up in the father, inflexible as the oaken hearts fashioned by his son.

Perhaps it was the offended pride of the father and the knowledge that his son enjoyed his schooling and excelled at it which made the decision so perverse. When Tomas was twelve, had just successfully completed sixth grade, was looking forward to completing his final two years of education and obtaining the certificate which announced his success, the father told him that he would not be returning to school in the fall. He was needed on the farm to feed the chickens, plant the vegetables, weed the truck patch, keep the house clean, and work at the woodshop, constructing the goods to be sold, bringing in the cash which would help to support them both.

Chapter 7   1921-1922

The Thursday I packed my knapsack and bedroll and left Newtown was my eighteenth birthday. I didn't think about it until later. The Turners, if they thought of me at all, assumed I was twenty, but when I left the town, walking north, I reclaimed my actual age. I didn't leave a note for Mr. Turner, but I believed he would understand when he saw the carved keepsake box, and Mrs. Turner would be glad I was gone. I felt bad about leaving Hank and his wife without saying anything to them, but I wouldn't know what to say or to tell them. The few townspeople and shopkeepers I had been acquainted with weren't friends, and I supposed my disappearance would give them all something to discuss during their times of inactivity.

I thought about returning and spending one last night in the bed in the apartment and not on the road under a tree, but feared I might change my mind about leaving if I went back. Without Ava, without our son, there was nothing left for me in Newtown. I needed to move on.

I walked until it was dark, and I couldn't see the time with the used pocket watch I had purchased at Mandy's, but I wasn't tired, and continued until I was. I didn't have any daylight to check carefully in the wooded area and make sure it was safe, but I found a small group of trees just off the side of the road, and settled there for the night. My mind wouldn't stop, and I found it difficult to sleep, but slowly I calmed down and closed my eyes.

A loud rooster at the nearby farm woke me. I did what was necessary behind the tree, gathered my things, looked around to see where I was, which was nowhere familiar, and continued to walk. I had taken the remainder of the lunch Mr. Turner left on the front table of the shop, and there were some sandwiches and apples and a few cookies, so I thought I could last the day with them. I needed to find another town to get supplies, and this time, because I had brought all the money I saved with me, I felt better prepared. I was older and knew that the seventy-eight dollars wouldn't last forever. I needed to get to a different town. I needed to find a job.

The day was cool for September, and that might be why I was able to move quicker and walk farther. I thought back to my first journey, when I had left the farm and my father, and it seemed a thousand years ago. So much had happened. As the farmhouses began to inch closer together, I knew a town was not too far, and tonight, if they had a small hotel, I would spend some money and stay in one. I wanted to clean up and shave and get a decent night's sleep before I started out again.

I don't remember the name of the first town, but it didn't seem very friendly, and although I stayed there one night, and ate a decent meal, cleaned myself, and got some sleep, I had no desire to remain. I left the next morning and after a breakfast at the town's restaurant, I purchased some foodstuffs at the general store. Then I shopped and spent additional money at a second-hand store. I obtained a larger knapsack, some necessary equipment for camping out, and added one more blanket to my bedroll which was worn and tattered. I walked out of the town, and once I was far enough away, I went into the woods where I would not be seen and reorganized my belongings. Taking the advice of my dead father, I separated and hid my remaining money in various carriers. I kept the change and three one-dollar bills in my pants pocket. I looked at the small compass on the end of the army soldier's knife I had picked up at the second-hand store and continued north.

***

I walked the remainder of September and October. There were a few times I met up with other travelers, and we would stay together and share stories. I reverted to the story about heading north to Chicago, or sometimes Wisconsin, because my father, or sometimes uncle or brother, had died, and I was going to meet up with my sister, or grandfather, or aunt. I didn't keep track of what I told anyone because I never saw them again. We would share what food we had and spend a night under some trees, not really trusting each other and sleeping poorly. And when one of us stopped at a town or took another road, no harm was done. I stopped shaving because it was too difficult to do without proper equipment and a mirror, and allowed my face a beard. Once I caught sight of myself in a pond and realized that the beard made me look older, and I liked the look. I appeared rugged and manly, and certainly not just eighteen years old.

I never told anyone I met my real name, but called myself Ned, or Frank, or, even Aaron, like my brother-in-law. Sometimes I would pick up a job here or there, helping a farmer throughout the day or even a couple days, earning a quarter or two and some hot meals, and sometimes sleeping in his barn, but never staying too long. One time I took a job for three days in a small town where the undertaker needed a casket made in a hurry. I was paid three dollars for my efforts and offered a permanent place there, but I didn't like the town, and the casket making brought back memories I would rather not keep, so I left.

I was headed northeast and crossed over to Kankakee County and found the towns there pleasant and the people friendly. There was a decent sized city called Bonneville, and I stopped there one afternoon because I needed a bath and a decent bed for the night. I had been walking for a while and thought I might settle somewhere. It was close to November and getting colder. Winter would be here, and I wondered if I could find a job and a place until spring. Bonneville seemed a better place than most, and I checked into a small hotel where the single rooms were cheap, not overly clean, but cleaner than a dirt floor, so I took a room and thought I would try out the town. I cleaned up and went looking for a barber. I got a haircut, but told him to shape the beard to my face. It was an advantage to look older.

Barbers know their towns. When I asked the one working on my beard about possible carpenter jobs or working at a furniture store, he squinched up his forehead and thought.

"Not sure about town, no shops like that here, but there is a lady, a Mrs. Vogel, who lives just a bit east of the town. I hear she's been looking for someone to do some kind of fence repairs, and if that's something you can do, there might be a job for you for a time."

He gave me directions, we spoke a bit, and I tipped him a dime.

"Thanks, Ned," he said, using my alias, "Good luck with the job-hunting!"

It was late, and I thought I would figure out where this Vogel house was in the morning. I found a place to grab some dinner; then went back to the cheap hotel and up to my room where I took out *The Tempest* and reread the story about magic and love. I fell asleep on a lumpy, but real bed.

I woke up when the sun came streaming through the window whose shade I couldn't pull down because it was broken. I dressed and thought I would stay one more night, so I went to tell the desk and then looked for some breakfast. As I ate the eggs and ham and drank the coffee, I started a conversation with the older woman who worked as a waitress. I figured she would know, so I asked about the Vogel place.

"It's out east of town and is a large house. You can't miss it because there's nothing else around. Mr. Vogel bought up the land around his place years ago, and I guess he meant to do something with it. He had the money, that's for sure."

"So he hasn't done anything with it yet?"

"Not likely. He died a few years back, and his widow lives there with a married couple who act as her housekeeper and gardener. We don't see her in town. Keeps to herself. She used to give singing lessons, but no one has taken any for years, not since the old man died. Too bad. I hear she had a nice voice."

I finished drinking the coffee, thanked the waitress, tipped her, and left. *Big spender*, I thought to myself, *my money will be gone soon if I don't get a job*. I wandered down the streets, looking in the shop windows, but it was early and nothing was open. I wondered what time would be appropriate to just appear at a house and ask about fixing a fence, and decided I would head east and look for the place. I took off my hat, shook it out, set it squarely back on my head, and began to search for the Vogel property, to find the Widow Vogel, to try to earn some money.

It was easy to find. The house was set back of the main road and surrounded by nothing but lots of land. There was what I assumed would be a fine garden in the warm months. Some outbuildings, including a large barn and what looked like a greenhouse, were behind it. A great wrap-around porch was visible, and even from the road, I could see that some of the balusters were broken, and at least one of the posts was down. They could be fixed, and I wondered what else there was to do that could earn me money. I walked up the stairs, avoiding the broken one, and lifted the very fine door knocker, dropping it three times. I was reminded of doing the very same thing when I was first at the Turner house, and a knot immediately appeared in my stomach.

I waited for a time, and had to knock again, and a woman I later learned was Mrs. Anderson, the housekeeper, finally came to the door. Later, I also learned that I should have used the back entrance, the one for workers and servants, and later still, in the coming winter months, when I remained safe and warm, I wondered which I would be considered.

She wasn't friendly. "We don't want to buy nothin' and already been Jesus-saved," I was told.

"Not here for that. I understand some fences need to be fixed, and I can see this porch needs looking after. I can do that. I'm a carpenter and a good one. Is the lady of the house here?"

Mrs. Anderson hesitated, and then said, "Wait here," and disappeared into the house. It took a time, but when she came back, she said, "Mrs. Vogel said if you can fix the porch, she'll pay you. There's other things to be done, but she wants to check out the job first." Then she looked me up and down and made the observation, "For a man needin' working tools, I don't see none. Lucky there's some in the outbuilding next to the barn. Go on around. I'll get my husband to open it for you. Mrs. Vogel said she'd pay a flat five dollars for the porch, and I'm to give you a meal. Come around the back when you're done. Take it or leave it."

I took it and thanked her. In the coming months, we would never be friends, but she would acknowledge my carpentry work as *decent*. As far as other activities, she gave a blind eye. I went around to the back and saw an older man, limping greatly and using a cane, head to a large shed. I met Mr. Anderson, and he opened the shed and pointed out the tools which were plentiful and of the highest caliber. Someone must have done some carpentry at one time, but looking at poor arthritic Mr. Anderson, I understood it wasn't him. There was extra wood in the back, and I could repair the step in the front, so I took off my jacket, even though it was a chilly November day, and got to work.

The repairs were easy, and I walked around the whole of the porch checking out additional problems, and tightening the loosened screws and railings and caps. Painting was needed, but that was not what I contracted for, and I thought I might be able to get another day of work from this job. It was late afternoon when I was finished, and I placed everything back, straightened out the shed, and looked around for paint. It was there, and I would offer to paint the next day.

I went around to the back and knocked on the door. Mrs. Anderson came and let me in. "Go on to the back summer kitchen. There's a bathroom there you can use to wash up, and I'll get a meal ready. Hope you like pork chops and cabbage 'cause it's what you're gettin'," and she pointed the way for me.

She was a great cook, and I tried not to make a pig of myself as I ate, but when she offered seconds, I took them. There was a sugar cream pie for dessert, and when I was done, I said, "Ma'am, that was as fine a meal as I can remember. Thank you. I don't know what your Missus wants done, but I can come back and paint the porch tomorrow if she would like me to. There's paint for it in the shed."

Mrs. Anderson took the plates from the table and then looked at me. "Let me put these in the sink and ask." She was gone a while and came back to say, "Mrs. Vogel would like to speak with you."

I got up, brushed off my pants and shirt, and she led me to what I would find out later was the back parlor. I stood off a bit while the housekeeper cleared her throat and said, "Mrs. Vogel, here's that workman," and then she left me alone with Ingrid Vogel.

I expected an old woman, perhaps bent in stature, and wrinkled in features, but I was taken back by the woman holding a book. She could not have been older than twenty-five (later I found out she was in her early thirties), and when I searched for the words to describe her, *refined* and *elegant* sprang to mind. Ingrid Vogel was not beautiful, but she had something more splendid than mere beauty, something cultured and majestic. Her skin was a dewy sweetness, a soft marble, and her hair was burnt umber, like a stain Mr. Turner and I once used. Her hair was long, giving an antique look to the knot piled upon her head. Her eyes matched her hair, and underneath her softness I detected a restlessness.

"I am sorry, but I don't know your name," she began.

I didn't give an alias. I did not lie to her then or after. I didn't want to. "Thomas, Ma'am. Thomas Allerton."

"You have done a fine job, Thomas Allerton. I inspected your work just now and am pleased with it. Mrs. Anderson informs me that you would be willing to paint the porch, and that would be fine. While the weather holds, and before snow sets in, I would like to have it done. Could you return tomorrow?"

"Yes, I will be here."

"Fine. Then tomorrow's pay will be the same. Please see Mrs. Anderson on your way out. She'll have your money. And, Mr. Allerton, do you do other repairs? There are some things around the house needing repairs, and I could probably keep you busy for a week or so."

"Yes, Ma'am. I'm a carpenter and furniture maker, and can help. Thank you for the work, Mrs. Vogel," and I left as she took up the book she had placed down, continuing to read.

Mrs. Anderson gave me the money as I left, and I said, "I'll be here in the morning for the painting," but she just answered "Hmph!"

I went back to the hotel and paid for another night. I felt wealthy. She had overpaid me, but I would not complain. Apparently, she had the money. The next morning, I was at the Vogel house by eight o'clock. The weather was chilly, but the painting would would not take that long. The same scene played out. Mrs. Anderson fed me (pounded steak and onions with mashed potatoes and carrots), took me to Mrs. Vogel, and I stood waiting for her pronouncement.

She was in the music room, looking through some sheet music as I stood there. When she noticed me, she smiled and said, "Mr. Allerton, the painting is carefully done. I appreciate the neat job. You said you could repair things, and the back fence needs repairing. There are also items in this house and around it which need attention. I will pay you five dollars a day for the work. Mr. Anderson has a list for you, and if you are in need of materials, let him know, and he will obtain them for you. Will that be acceptable?"

It was more than acceptable, and I said, "Yes, Mrs. Vogel. I can begin on the other things tomorrow," and I left to see Mr. Anderson.

That was how it started. There was mending to be done to the back fencing and some of the wood furniture in the house needed work. While much of it was easy, there were some tricky repairs to items which were obviously a century or so old. From what I gathered, Mr. Vogel came from Germany, settled in this area with the lovely things he had sent over from Europe, and married a youthful Ingrid. After half a dozen years together, he died, leaving a rich widow. Ingrid had been musically trained at some college in the east, and was singing at an Opera House in New York when Mr. Vogel, who was visiting friends there, saw and heard her. And then married her. I knew nothing more about her youth or past life and never asked. She was not the kind of woman to speak of those things, and I was shy about inquiring.

I began to work there as a regular job. Each morning I would wake and walk out to the house, complete my work, eat a delicious meal prepared by Mrs. Anderson, and at late afternoon, walk back to the cheap hotel where I spent the night. Then, it would begin again. The weather was growing colder and a few snow flurries surrounded my head as I walked home each evening. One afternoon, as I was working in an upstairs bedroom, repairing the frame for a large four-poster bed, I looked out the window and saw that the flurries had become a storm and there was a half-foot of snow on the ground. It would be a miserable and difficult walk home, and I was not looking forward to it. I left soon after that, but was stopped by Mrs. Anderson at the back door.

"Mr. Allerton, Mrs. Vogel asked me to remind you that tomorrow is Thanksgiving feast day, and she is not expecting you to work until Monday. Also, she wanted me to send home this dinner for you," and she handed me a large wrapped parcel.

I had forgotten the date. I thought back to one year ago and the Turner's feast and the joy I had with Ava, and swallowed hard. I took the parcel and said, "Thank you, Mrs. Anderson. And please thank Mrs. Vogel for me. I'll be back on Monday," and, wrapping my scarf, the one Ava knit for me, around my neck, I left.

On Monday, as I trudged through the snow to get to the house, I wondered how long this job would last. The walk was not bad in the decent weather, but the snow continued to come down, and I was frozen by the time I arrived. I stood at the back of the house and removed my wet coat and stamped off my boots and dried them with the rag given to me by Mrs. Anderson. I walked into the back of the kitchen and was surprised to see Mrs. Vogel seated at the long table

"Mr. Allerton. Please sit down. I wish to speak to you. Mrs. Anderson, please bring him some coffee, and I will have another cup."

I sat down, assuming I was being told I was done, and was being dismissed. I thanked Mrs. Anderson when she brought the coffee, and sipped at the hotness while I waited for Mrs. Vogel to speak.

"Where do you stay at night, Mr. Allerton?"

"I have a room in the small hotel in town."

"What is your story? Where are you from, and why are you traveling around? You are obviously talented and skilled, and could easily find a job in one of the larger towns."

I didn't lie. I answered her questions. "I was married and my wife and newborn son died earlier this year. There was nothing left for me in that town, and I needed to leave, so I have been traveling and picking up a job here and there. I could, and at some time, probably will settle down somewhere, but for now, I'm happy with the way I'm living."

She took a sip of her coffee and looked down at the cup for a few seconds before she spoke. "Winter has come, and winters here are bleak and stark. I would like to make a proposal. There are many bedrooms in this large house. The Andersons live in the back where there is a three-room suite for them. Would you consider moving here for the winter and accept staying in one of the third-floor rooms? That would save you the cold walk twice a day, and it would make it more convenient for you to complete the work. Besides, I am thinking of adding a new side table to the dining room and a small bookcase in the front parlor, and you being here would make accomplishing that easier. I fully understand if you would prefer not to."

I looked at her. Then I smiled. "Yes, Mrs. Vogel, that would be acceptable to me."

"Fine," she said, "Then tomorrow when you arrive for work, bring your things, and Mrs. Anderson will show you to your room." She got up from the table, and I also rose. As she left, she turned to ask one more thing, "Mr. Allerton, how old are you?"

I wiped my sweaty hands on my pants. And again, I told the truth. "I'm eighteen."

"Eighteen," she repeated, and left the room.

And I moved in.

***

I cannot account for the actions of either of us over the next months. Sometimes, it seems a dream. I settled into a comfortable third-floor bedroom, and Mrs. Anderson's attitude was unmistakable. She didn't approve, but she had nothing to say, being a servant in the house. She reminded me of Mrs. Turner, and I hid my grin when she *hmphed* around me, making sure I heard. Within a few weeks, all the inside repairs had been made, the side table and small bookcase completed, and the first time I came down the stairs in the morning and realized that there was no real work for me, I panicked and thought it would be a cold and miserable walk to town. But Mrs. Vogel asked to see me, and I was taken to the library, a room I had not visited because no repairs were needed there. I walked in, and the small-town rube in me came out. Mrs. Vogel was seated at a large desk reading a book. She saw me look about the room, and smiled.

"My husband was a collector of fine books," she said, "although he wasn't much of a reader. I am, and from what Mrs. Anderson tells me, you have a few books of your own. Do you enjoy reading, Mr. Allerton?"

"I do. I own three books which I reread. They were given to me by a teacher when I was younger. This is amazing," and I slowly walked up and down the bookcases, well built from mahogany, and looked at the titles. Some were in foreign languages, but the ones in English called to me. I could hardly keep from grabbing them to look through the pages, to gather the words into me.

"Mr. Allerton, I am inviting you to take and read whatever you want. These books are wasting away here, for lack of use. I often spend afternoons and early evenings reading and would enjoy your company. It is good to read and discuss, and I know that, for now, there are few further repairs needed. The winter is here, and the fireplace in the back parlor is kept lit and warms the room. I hope you will join me there later with a book you have chosen."

I was too excited to be embarrassed, and nodded in agreement as I came across dozens of slim volumes of Shakespeare plays. I took out one I hadn't read, *Much Ado About Nothing*, and opened it up.

"Ah, you read Shakespeare. Have you read many plays?"

"Only two. I have a copy of *The Tempest* and have read *Julius Caesar*, but I would like to read this, if you don't mind."

"Please, Mr. Allerton. This library is open for your use. I haven't read that play in a while, so when you are finished, I'll reread it, and we might discuss it."

And so the reading started.

***

We met together twice a day, the early afternoon, and the evenings, and while I felt awkward and anxious at first, soon I was at ease. We read silently, and periodically, because a certain passage needed it, read aloud to each other. We discussed the Shakespeare plays I read, and sometimes a novel or an essay. A freedom and casualness, an informality surrounded us, and we became almost friends. I say *almost* because we were not. I was unsure of my place in the house, but didn't spend time worrying about it. I simply accepted my fortune.

I took my meals in the kitchen by myself, and one evening, as I was getting ready to go there and see what delight Mrs. Anderson had left for me on the stove, Mrs. Vogel stopped me.

"Mr. Allerton, it is silly for us to be apart at mealtime when we spend so much of the day together. Please have your meals with me in the dining room. We can continue our discussions. There is no reason for us to be so formal."

So that is what we did. I felt uncomfortable at first, but soon, just like the reading, I became relaxed, and we continued our discussions.

She asked me questions about myself and my background, and I told
her the story of my life. She was the only woman with whom I was
so immediately forthright and honest. I never lied to her. There was
something about her that encouraged my veracity. I told her about living
with Aunt Jennifer, and then my move to the farm with my father, and
the work I did in the woodshop. I expressed my joy at schooling, and my
sorrow when I could not continue it. I told her about my mother I barely
remembered, the twin brother I had never known, and about leaving my
father when he was dying, and my travels and experiences on the road.
I cried when I described Ava and my son, and how Mr. Turner was the
father-figure I wanted, and that Mrs. Turner needed to be rid of me. I
made her laugh with my stupidity. And I laughed at it too.

The Christmas season came and then the New Year of 1922,
and although Prohibition was the law of the land, all of us, Mr. and Mrs.
Anderson included, celebrated, and drank many toasts of a sparkling
wine, and laughed at silliness. I had not had wine before, and was
amazed at how sparkling I felt. I was unprepared the next morning
when I felt ill, and Mrs. Vogel just laughed and asked Mrs. Anderson
to bring me black coffee and dry toast. We settled into the winter and
when the weather permitted, Mrs. Vogel and I went for walks along the
silent paths of some wooded areas and remarked upon the animal tracks
we found. The days passed, and I was content, and she seemed happy.
Happy enough that sometimes she played the piano and sang for me, and
her voice was as lovely as she looked, and I was grateful for my good
fortune, and ignored what would happen in the coming spring.

One cold evening, after we shared an evening meal, we sat and
read out loud to each other until it was time for bed. I closed my book
and wished her a good-night. She said she was going to remain in the
parlor for a time and finish her reading, so I walked up to my room,
cleaned up, and went to bed.

The room was dark and the softness of the snow fell against
the window which was across from my bed, and I felt comforted. I was
asleep when I felt someone next to me, and it startled me awake. When
I turned and saw I shared my bed with Mrs. Vogel, I thought I was
dreaming, but when I began to say something to her (what I was going to
say, I had no idea), she put her finger to my mouth, shook her head, and
said "Shh!"

After that, no words were required. I was shocked, but that only
lasted for a brief, a very brief, time. I almost expected this to happen,
and I accepted it exactly as I had accepted the room in the house, and the

books in my hand, and the meals in the dining room. We never spoke, and after an hour or two, I fell asleep again. And I did not dream.

That was the first night-time visit.

***

Sometime in the night, she left because I was alone when I awoke. I thought that it was a dream at first, but conceded it wasn't. I readied myself to go downstairs, unsure how I would face Mrs. Vogel, what I would do or say. What *would* I be expected to do or say? I walked slowly down the three flights of stairs and slowly into the dining room where she was seated at the table.

"Good morning, Mr. Allerton, I trust you slept well. Mrs. Anderson, please bring breakfast now," and with those words, everything was normal.

We continued through the day without any acknowledgement of the previous night's activities, and I began to think I did dream it all. We sat and read and discussed and then walked for a while outside, although a rapid snow began, and we didn't remain outside for long. Dinner that night was delicious, and Mrs. Vogel and I went to the music room where she sang and played the piano until it was time to stop. I wished her a good-night and went to my room.

I had fallen asleep and was awakened again some hours later. Mrs. Vogel, her burnt umber hair down around her shoulders, and her nightdress on the floor beside my bed, slipped her arms around me, and I turned to her. In the darkness and the comfort of the night, we found a different alliance, a link, a correlation. And I knew this was not a dream.

She never stayed the night. I never knew when she would come into my bed, and some nights, she didn't. We never spoke, and the one time I held her back as she was leaving, I whispered, "Stay," and she whispered back, "No."

Our days were as they had been. We ate meals together and laughed and read and discussed and walked. And the nights when she visited were filled with silent passion and never spoken about during the light. I was living two different lives. So was she. I was young and relatively inexperienced, but the connection we had was strong and vibrant, and taught me in a way distinguishable from the teachings of the books, and I wondered if this would continue when spring arrived.

February snow came, and March rains melted it, and one day, I awoke to the singing of birds. When I looked out my window, crocus dotted the side of the house, and change had come. For the past three nights I had slept alone, and while our days continued as they had previously, I was wary and waiting.

I went downstairs to the dining room, but she wasn't there, and the dining table wasn't set for breakfast. I heard Mrs. Anderson in the kitchen, and when I came in, she turned to me, and barely hiding the pleasure from her tone, spoke.

"Have a seat. Mrs. Vogel wants you to have a good breakfast before you leave. She thanks you for your service and work. There's an envelope with the remainder of your pay on the table, and once you get your stuff packed, Mr. Anderson will drive you back to town. Want pancakes or eggs?"

I didn't want either, and told her I would just take a cup of coffee and asked if I could speak to Mrs. Vogel.

"Sorry, she don't want to be disturbed."

I drank the coffee standing up, took the envelope from the table, and shoved it into my pocket before I went back up the stairs. I hesitated on the second floor, near her bedroom, but the door was closed, and no sounds could be heard, and I wasn't brave enough to knock. What would I say? Had I done something wrong? What was happening? Was she angry? There were no answers, and I decided that I wanted out of the house. I went to my room, packed everything, and came back down the stairs. Mr. Anderson was waiting for me by the horse and wagon, and I threw my things in the back and climbed in beside him. Mrs. Anderson was nowhere to be found. I did not tell her good-bye.

He pulled out of the side path which was spring-muddy, and we drove to town. As he turned the corner onto the main road, I looked back at the house, back to the second floor to the bedroom window which I knew was hers. I watched it until the wagon made the turn to town, but there was no movement behind it. No stirring or shifting of the curtain hanging there. It remained mute and immobile.

Mr. Anderson did not speak and neither did I. In my months at the house, I had rarely spoken to him, and there was nothing to say at this point. It did not take long to get to the town, and before he entered the main street, I asked him to stop and proceeded to get down from the wagon. I reached into the back to gather my belongings, and as I thanked him, he took out a package and handed it to me. Then he turned and left. I watched him travel back down the road, back to the house where I assumed he would care for the crocus plants whose blooms would only last about three weeks.

It was almost midday. I was hungry. I walked to a small restaurant, sat in a back booth, and ordered a sandwich and coffee. As I waited and took stock of what was next for me, I remembered the envelope in my pocket. I removed in and held it under the table and opened it. It contained one-hundred dollars in small bills. I placed it back, deep into my pocket.

When the waitress brought the food, I ate and deliberated. It was time to move on. I would travel towards Chicago since I was headed in that direction. I sipped at the coffee, waved away the waitress when she offered more, and took up the package Mr. Anderson had handed me. It was wrapped in brown paper and tied with string, but I felt it and knew it was a book. I unwrapped the paper, and the title proclaimed: *The Sonnets of Shakespeare*. There was a slip of paper at the place where *Sonnet 73* was located. I had never read a sonnet. I didn't even understand what a sonnet was, but the last two lines read:

This thou perceiv'st, which makes thy love more strong,

To love that well which thou must leave ere long.

I didn't know what they meant or what the sonnet said, but I would try to figure it out. The lines had been underlined. I knew she had underlined them for me.

I put the book into my larger knapsack, paid my tab, and left. Before I started on the road, I visited the barber shop I had been to months before. The man I had spoken to during my first visit wasn't there, but I instructed the barber who asked me what I wanted to cut my hair and shave off my beard. I didn't need to look older. I was older.

Sonnet 73

That time of year thou mayst in me behold

When yellow leaves, or none, or few, do hang

Upon those boughs which shake against the cold,

Bare ruined choirs, where late the sweet birds sang.

In me thou see'st the twilight of such day

As after sunset fadeth in the west;

Which by and by black night doth take away,

Death's second self, that seals up all in rest.

In me thou see'st the glowing of such fire,

That on the ashes of his youth doth lie,

As the death-bed, whereon it must expire,

Consumed with that which it was nourish'd by.

This thou perceiv'st, which makes thy love more strong,

To love that well, which thou must leave ere long.

Chapter 8   1909

Tomas was not yet two years old when his mother died, and he went to stay with his Aunt Jennifer and Uncle David and their three children. His cousins were older, but the younger one sometimes played with him after school. His maternal grandmother who had moved in with Jennifer's family when her husband died, was alive and not yet so senile that she didn't recognize him and note his resemblance. "Oh child, you have your poor mother's face," she would say, and hold him and weep until he struggled for freedom. Tomas avoided her and ran from her which increased her weeping.

Tomas saw his father on the rare Sundays when he came to have dinner with his in-laws. Jennifer told her brother-in-law that he was welcome every Sunday, and she hoped to see him at church where he was invited to sit with them in the family pew, even though she was aware of his disinclination for religion. Periodically, Tomas' Uncle David would drive out to the farm to visit as the father worked in the woodshop. Tomas was always happy to ride with his uncle in the automobile. He wasn't as happy to see his father who looked at him and rumpled his hair and thought that this son, the only living one of the four born to him and his dead wife, was being spoiled and needed a more rigorous upbringing. He would see to it when he brought the boy back to the farm to live. That happened when Tomas was almost six.

Late summer, after Tomas had spent four years with his aunt's family, his father determined it was time for him to return to the farm. One morning, after the horse had been hitched to the wagon and the cedar chest the father had been contracted to make for one of the families in town was delivered, he stopped by Jennifer's house. Tomas was playing in the yard. He looked up to see who was disturbing him and ran into the house when he saw his father. The man pulled back on the horse's reins, stopped, and got down from the seat. As he walked up the front steps, his sister-in-law came out and greeted him while his son peeked out from behind the screen door.

"Good morning! Didn't expect you today. Come on in and have some coffee. I'm just finishing up some cookies, and they're ready for tasting. David is at the office, but I expect him home for lunch in an hour or so if you would like to wait for him. You are welcome to have lunch here."

The boy's father removed his hat in deference to womanhood in general, not to this one specifically. He shook his head.

"Thanks, but I need to get back and finish up some things. I just came by to get my son. It's time for him to live with me, and if you would pack his things, I'd appreciate it."

He stood there and looked at Jennifer and then glanced at Tomas who wasn't sure exactly what was happening but knew his life was about to change. He knew this man was his *father*, but after four years living at this house, he assumed it was just a word, not a relationship.

Jennifer looked at her brother-in-law, the man she had never forgiven for her sister, Clara's, death. She swallowed and said, "Please come in. Let's talk and have some coffee. I need to check on my cookies," and she quickly walked back into the house, instructing Tomas to go to his room and play. She didn't wait for her brother-in-law, giving him no chance to refuse her. He followed her into the house and into the kitchen.

Jennifer busied herself with the cookies and poured some coffee for her guest. She placed half a dozen sweets on a plate which was put on the table. Then she poured herself a cup and sat down across from him. She poured milk into her cup, stirred, and took a sip before facing him.

"Tomas is not yet six. He won't go to school for another year, and if you move him to your farm, you would need to watch after him. Leave him here until he begins school. Don't you think that's what Clara would have wanted? He's happy here, and we enjoy having him. Of course, he is yours, but he's still young and another year here won't hurt."

Her brother-in-law did not move. He did not drink the coffee or take a cookie. He let her speak. Then he did.

"Clara is no longer here, and I will make decisions about Tomas. He needs to learn from me, and now, before he begins his schooling, is the time to do that. He will be six this fall, and while I appreciate you taking him in while he was so young, he is no longer a baby. He will come home with me today. Please pack his things," and he got up from the table. "I'll wait in the wagon."

He turned to walk away, but stopped at the kitchen entrance and faced Jennifer. "I don't want you and David to think I'm ungrateful for all you've done. I appreciate it, and I know Clara would too. But Tomas is my son. I was trained by my grandfather at Tomas' age. He needs to learn, and I need the help," and he continued out the front door.

Jennifer held back tears. She wouldn't cry in front of this man. She supposed he was right, and she had always known that the time would come when Tomas would return to the farm and his father. She didn't know how she would give up this child who looked so like her sister. Perhaps David would come home earlier and talk to him. She would take her time packing up Tomas' clothes and toys. She began to wrap up the baked cookies to send home with the child. There would be no sweets for him at the farm.

***

At first, Tomas cried at night, but when the dog, Molly, crawled into the bed to comfort him, he stopped. He assumed this visit would be a short one, and soon, very soon, his real family would come and get him and return him to his second-floor bedroom where all the toys this father said he had to leave behind were located. But after a couple months, when he turned six, he began to understand that this would be his home. It was not nearly as nice as his real home. The house was not as large or ornately decorated or smelled of baking cookies and delicious meals. It was stark in its plainness with the one exception being two flowery aprons which had belonged to his mother, and hung on a hook in the kitchen. They rested against the wall. Mementos. Tomas did not remember his mother, and the photographs shown to him by his Aunt Jennifer did not stir his memory. She remained a glimmer.

He did not know his father either, having spent little time with him over the past four years, so he did not regard him at first with any negativity. That came later. The father, having had little to do with people, during the previous four years especially, had retreated into solitary essence, existing in reflections, resentments, and regrets. He did not know how to manage a young child, so he treated his son as he would an adult. Whatever conversations there were, kept to specifics and succinctness, and soon enough, Tomas learned that questions were not encouraged and answers, if given, were concise and curt. Tomas leaned to follow instructions, and the few times he did not, such as the time he was expected to drown the bag of new-born kittens, a swift slap was his recompence.

One day, during his first fall on the farm, the father spoke to him during breakfast and announced that they would be walking to the family gravesite to clean away the weeds and growths from the stones there. Tomas, who didn't remember cemeteries, and except for the burial of his mother when he was not yet two, and his grandmother a couple years ago, did not know what to expect. But he did know not to inquire. After the bowl of leftover groats was scraped into Molly's bowl, and the dishes were washed, the two of them went out to the barn and gathered tools to complete the task and began a walk to the edge of the property, close to the wooded area, where the dead family lay. Tomas had never been out this way, and was surprised when his father spoke to him as they walked.

"Your grandparents and my grandparents are out there. So are your brothers who are buried next to your mother. And my aunt, my father's sister, is there too."

Tomas was astounded. He hadn't known there were brothers. No one had ever mentioned this expanded family to him. He wanted to ask questions but wasn't sure where to start and was a bit fearful of saying the wrong thing, so he remained quiet. He father continued.

"My mother died when I was two, just like yours did, and my father died when I was six, your age now. I spent most of the time with my grandparents here at this farm and just continued to live with them. My grandfather was the best man around. He taught me everything I know."

Having been given this information, Tomas sifted through the sudden questions in his mind. He was too apprehensive to inquire about his close family: his mother and brothers, so he chose a safe question. "What about your aunt? I didn't know you had one."

"She died young. I never knew her. Her name was Dorothy."

They continued walking and Tomas decided to keep other questions until they were there in the hopes they would be answered. It didn't take long before they came to an area where nine stones were scattered under a copse of small prairie crabapple trees. The trees' fruit had dropped, creating a rotting mess. The father handed a rake to Tomas and told him to rake the rotting fruits away from the graves. They worked for a while, and Tomas tried his best, but the rake was too large for him to handle, and he struggled with it. However, his father did not complain or yell at him, but allowed the boy to teach himself the proper way.

When most of the apples were moved away, Tomas was shown how to pull up the large weeds which were surrounding the stones. As they worked, he asked, "Father, who is buried around here?"

The father stood up and stretched out his back. Tomas did also, and they stood there as the father pointed and answered.

"Here are my parents, your grandparents. Over there are my grandparents, and Dorothy is next to them. Your mother is buried here and these three small stones are your brothers."

Tomas looked at the small stones under which his ghostly siblings slept and asked, "I can't read. What are their names?"

"This one wasn't given a name. It just says *Son*. The other two were named *Edward*."

"Both of them?"

"Yes. They were given the same name although they were born different years," and he looked up to the sky which had darkened. "We better get back. Looks like rain. Pick up that rake and carry it back. There are still things you can help with in the woodshop today. One of the caskets needs sanding, and I'll show you what to do."

The two of them walked back to the main farm, put the tools away, and went to the woodshop where they worked the rest of the day. Tomas was beginning to enjoy the tasks in the shop. Other than directions or scoldings, there was no conversation, and he realized what he was doing was considered *work*, but it made him feel grown up. There were days the the sun was a perfect yellow orb and the sky claimed white softness, and he wished he were back at his real home, playing in the yard or sitting on the porch swing or busying himself with the toys in his bedroom. But in his core, he realized those times were gone, replaced by sanding, and feeding the chickens, and drying the dishes, and he accepted this new life. What other choice was there?

***

A year passed, and his days fell into a pattern. Up early, feed the chickens, complete the morning tasks, eat a morning meal, and get to the schoolhouse to learn. Tomas enjoyed his schooling and realized he had a knack for learning. He excelled at arithmetic, and reading opened a new world to him. He practiced by reading everything he could find, becoming expert at it.

When, during the following summer, right before he would turn eight in the fall, he was given a morning to run free, he visited the crabapple copse where his family rested. He was able to read out the initialed tombstones of his relatives, and his dead brothers, and their dates for himself. He pulled up a few weeds, and starting with his great-grandparents' stones, he walked from one to the other listing the letters and dates out loud. He came to the grave of his mother and three dead brothers. He recited the names and dates: *Son 1901*; *Edward 1902, Edward 1903*. He looked at the last date again and thought about it. That was the same year he had been born. His birthyear was also 1903. It was then, standing under the flowering trees, the sky an azure blue, the sun resplendent and glorious, that he realized the second *Edward*, the one placed right next to his mother, Clara, was not just his brother, but was his twin.

Chapter 9   1922-1923

I walked in the spring and was glad for it. At times, I met other travelers and enjoyed spending time with them, listening to their stories. I told some of my own, mostly made up. I never told others my real story. Apart from one person, and that was years later, I never told anyone I had been married; that I was a father. I especially never shared the story of Mrs. Vogel. I never mentioned my time with her. I wondered about her. I dreamed about her. But, I could not, would not, talk about her. She was a serendipitous circumstance that was mine alone. I reread and pondered Sonnet 73, and I think I figured out what she meant for me to understand about our time together. Of the four books I had then, and of all the books I have obtained since, the book she gave me was, and is, the most cherished.

Once I left Bonneville, I found a solitary wooded area and divided up my money. There was more of it, and I needed to keep it safe. Traveling the roads, sleeping outside, eating store crackers and wild berries were second nature now. I walked and stopped and walked again. Sometimes I stayed at a town's cheap hotel, and sometimes a farmer allowed me his barn for the night. I never took without asking or offering to work for it. Most of the time, I was outside, under some trees at night. Once I spend an entire week by a pond catching and eating the fish which I cooked over fires. It was pleasant there, and I considered making it my home for a longer time. But after a week, I was done, and I packed up and continued to walk.

I went northward. I knew I was close to Chicago but there were many small towns and cities to visit. I kept hearing about one place, an expanding city where there was work to be found and excitement to be had. It was called *Stone City*. There were limestone quarries and steel mills, and factories producing all sorts of items: horseshoes, bricks, cans, cars. I was positive there would be a need for a carpenter, so I headed that way and planned to find a job and a place to stay. Winter was coming, and I didn't want to be caught out in the snow and wind. I needed to be settled before that. I had a few months. September had passed. I had let my beard grow again because looking older was sometimes an advantage. And I was nineteen years old.

I found the city, a city of almost forty thousand, and many of them plain working people like me. The place was huge. Along with factories, there were dozens of shops, and even a college. I wandered the streets for a time, always conscious of the money I had stacked in my knapsack and roll and not sure if I was safe. I would have been more worried if I hadn't seen other men carrying their lives on their backs. I decided I needed to find a hotel to check into, and this time, I wasn't looking for a cheap one but a safe one.

I stopped at a restaurant to get a meal. The place looked decent enough, and there were a few men who carried knapsacks like me. I sat at the counter, stashing my belongings under my feet, and nodded to the man next to me. I ordered coffee and the Blue-Plate Special and listened to the talk around me. The meal came, and I began to eat. When I saw the man next to me spread the ketchup over his meatloaf, I asked if he would pass the bottle, and I did the same.

"Tastes better this way," I remarked, and the man nodded as he chewed. "Been here long?" I asked.

He swallowed and answered, "No, just a week. Staying at a hotel and just got a job today at one of the factories on the next street. Start tomorrow," and he took another bite. "If you're looking for work, they're hiring," he offered.

"Really? I am, so where is it?"

He named the place and where it was, and I thanked him.

"I need a place to stay, I guess. Just got into town and not sure which hotels are safest. Got any suggestions?"

The man swallowed his coffee and motioned for the waitress to refill his cup before he answered. "Stay away from the places on Wells Street. Heard they are filled with bedbugs and will cheat you in a sec. I got me a bed at the Stafford, about three streets up and on the left. Not the best, but it's clean and if you're willing to pay a bit more, you can have your own room. Small, but it'll do. They also rent by the week which is a better deal than by the night."

"Thanks. Good to know. Not sure I can afford a single room, but I'll check into it. Name's Tom," and I held out my hand and he shook it.

"Ben. Maybe I'll see you then. Got to get going. Told this girl I would meet her in an hour, and want to clean up. So long, Tom," and he left.

I wondered if I could trust him, but I had to take a chance, so I paid for the meal, shouldered my things, and went to the suggested hotel to check it out. The Stafford was suitable. I decided I didn't want to have a roommate and paid the extra for a week in a single room. I signed the register, took my key, and walked up the three flights of stairs.

I was tired and needed to clean up before I left in the morning to look for a job, so I waited my turn at the shared bathroom and then went back to the room. I looked at myself in the small mirror above the narrow table and knew I needed to find a barber in the morning. Hair needed cutting and beard needed trimming. I went about hiding some money, placing things under the thin mattress and in the small closet at the top shelf in the back, and in the toe of my extra shoes, and when I was done, without reading any sonnets, I went to sleep.

I was lucky. There was a furniture manufacturing company looking for workers. I applied and was given the job. The furniture business was different than what I was used to, and hand-made furniture like my father crafted, had given way to factory-made things. Not as good, in my estimation, but once I was hired and trained, and caught on to what was expected from me and how to run the machines, I was fine. This place made various pieces of furniture: tables and chairs, rockers, and bedframes; they were shipped to a big warehouse in Chicago and sold through catalogs from stores like Sears, Roebuck and Montgomery Ward. I learned a new way of working. It was a job and paid good money, and at least I could support myself. I was content with a job and a place to stay.

And I met a friend. Ben Nowak, the man I met at the restaurant, was staying at the Stafford, and we ran into each other one morning as we were leaving for work. He was an upright person who was amiable and kindly, and when we had time, we would walk the streets of Stone City, looking at the buildings and businesses, and then grab something to eat at a close-by diner. The girl he was meeting the day I met him turned into his steady girlfriend, and when I met Helen, she was down-to-earth and friendly. Sometimes the three of us would go out to eat or to a movie, but I felt strange butting in on their dates. One night the three of us were walking home from a movie, and Helen asked me if I wanted to meet someone.

"She's really great, Tom. I just met her because she moved into my boarding house, and we get along. She's a lot of fun and maybe a bit wild, but I think you'd like her. Come on; the four of us can do things together, and you won't be so lonely. What do you say?"

I was lonely, so I told her that would be fine; I would meet her friend. The following Saturday, after work, Ben and I cleaned up and walked over to the boarding house where Helen and her friend were staying. We waited in the small parlor downstairs, because men weren't allowed up to the rooms. We watched the building elevator make two stops on the main floor, leaving its passengers out: women meeting their dates, or others, arm-in-arm, leaving the building, laughing and ready for some fun. On the elevator's third trip, behind the crowd of additional fun-seekers, Helen and her friend exited the elevator and walked towards us.

***

She was called *Belle*. Isabella Garnier was her name, but everyone called her *Belle*. There was a flair about her, a flirtiness and playfulness which appealed to me, and I liked her right away. She looked different than many of the other girls, including Helen. Helen was cute, but she looked like most of the other women who had gotten off the elevator. Her hair was cut in a bob, and her dress was the typical flapper-style. Belle didn't dress like that, and her hair was uncut. It was dark, almost black, and curly. She told me once that she had tried to straighten it with some sort of iron, but it wouldn't stay straight, and she didn't have the money to get it done professionally, so she just left it, and pulled it back out of her face. It was usually tied with a red ribbon because red was her favorite color. She wore trousers. I had never seen a woman wearing them except for some of the fancy movie stars that were in the films I saw, but she looked great in them. Later, I discovered she made all her own clothes and was a decent seamstress. She looked and dressed the way she wanted, and I guess that appealed to me. Helen had said she was a bit wild. But I didn't learn how wild until later.

The four of us went to a theater and saw *The Valley of Silent Men,* which was a fine film. It was a romance for the girls and a mystery for me, and Ben didn't care much for it at all, but I think that was because the reel broke at one of the best parts, and we had to wait until it was fixed. After the movie, we walked to Coop's Café and ate. We all ordered the veal loaf with tomato sauce and mashed potatoes and drank ginger ale. Belle made us laugh with her impressions of some of the women at the boarding house. She was a natural actress, and we laughed so loudly a woman who was leaving the café with her husband looked at us and said, "Well, I never…!" When she left, Belle perfectly mimicked her, and we laughed some more. Ben said he knew someone at his job who could let him know of a speakeasy in the neighborhood, so we made plans to go there the following Saturday. We walked the girls back to their boarding house, and to my surprise, Belle reached up and kissed my cheek when we left.

"Say, Belle seems great. Don't you like her?"

"She is great," I answered, "I was just surprised by her. She's fun, and I do like her."

Back at the Stafford, Ben and I said good-night, and we went up to our rooms. I got ready for bed and laid down to think about the evening. I fell asleep, and that was the first night in a long time that I didn't dream about Mrs. Vogel.

***

She was fun, and I was taken by her. She was exotic in her looks and wasn't afraid of anything. She would dare me to walk along the curbs and not fall; she frightened me when she took chances and walked backwards in oncoming traffic and laughed when drivers honked at her; she would run in her trousers and jump over puddles of water, not always making it across, but was amused at the wetness creeping up her trouser pants legs. She liked to drink, and when Ben did get us into a speakeasy, she gulped down a gin rickey immediately, before the rest of us even took a few sips. And she loved to dance. She was never afraid to look different in her trousers and long beads and wild curly hair which always came loose, and she didn't need me or anyone else to be her partner. Belle would dance by herself and have a great time doing it.

Belle worked at one of the garment factories sewing skirts and blouses, and she was an expert at operating the sewing machine. There was one at the boarding house, and she used it to make her clothes. She talked about owning her own dress shop and making the kind of finery she said women wanted, the kind she made and wore herself. Sometimes she wore a dress, but Belle's dresses were always shorter and deeper cut than most. She was never afraid to look different, even wearing a dress. She told me that one day she wanted to visit France because her grandparents were from there, and she spoke a bit of French which added to her exoticness.

"Mon cheri, qu-est-ce que tu penses? C`est formidable, n`est-ce pas?" she would ask me as she twirled around and laughed when I didn't understand her.

She had moved to Stone City with her mother, Blanche, and sister, Bertha, after her father died, but I didn't know she had any relatives living close to her. Not in the beginning. She and her mother fought over many things, and Belle decided to move out of the small apartment they all shared and into the boarding house where she claimed she could live as she wanted. And she did. She dressed and acted and spent her money in her own way. She laughed and made me laugh. She took chances that often frightened me, but she was unafraid, and I found her captivating and bewitching, and thought I was in love with her. I told her so, and when she hugged me and laughed and whispered, *"Mon cheri, on fait l`amour?"*, I didn't understand the language, but I knew what she meant.

***

I spent some of my secreted money on her at Christmas. I searched out and bought her some of the *artificial silk* that was popular and which she wanted. She planned to create a specially designed dress for our evenings out. I got the material in the red color she loved and found some matching sparkly hair clips for her wild hair. I told her that when the winter weather cleared enough for her to wear her gossamer, sheer dress, we would have a fancy dinner and go to our favorite speakeasy and dance all night. But the gift I spent the most care on, the thing that didn't cost me money but only my expertise and time, was a carved wooden heart which could be held in the palm of her hand. Into the heart I chiseled a dozen small individual hearts so the entire creation was a heart made of hearts. I wanted her to know how much she meant to me and how happy I was with her.

She was thrilled and delighted with it all, and I waited for her to tell me the dress was made and give me the go-ahead to plan our special evening out. January passed, and February left, and we continued to have fun, but I knew that in spring, once the snow was gone and she could go out in the stylish red dress she would create, not needing to cover it up with a winter coat, she would. March passed, then April, and when May came, I finally asked her about the dress.

"Belle, that dress you are making must really be something. It's been months, and I haven't seen it yet. Are you almost finished with it?"

She was quieter than usual, and when she looked at me, there was a conspiratorial smile on her lips. She came close to me and took my arm and looked up into my face when she said, "Ah, cheri, I believe I may be working on making something else. Something you have helped me make," and that was how I found out I would once again be a father.

Chapter 10   1905

The office in his home was at the back of the first floor, the only window facing the back yard and the wooded area, and no one could see in, but Doctor Warin shut the drapery anyway before he injected the hypodermic syringe filled with half a grain of morphine into his left back thigh. He was tired, his head ached, his arthritic hip was acting up, and this seemed to relieve him faster than the laudanum drops in wine. Besides, Mrs. Warin was expert at smelling his breath, and he didn't have time for an argument. He was too busy. He had three stops and then needed to get out to the Allerton farm to see Clara. Poor thing. She suffered so with those failed pregnancies, and he knew the bottles of laudanum he had given her last month were most likely gone by now. He made sure his bag was packed, grabbed his hat, duster, and goggles, and snuck out the side door, avoiding Mrs. Warin.

Earlier in the year, Doctor Warin bought a Ford Model C, a *Doctor's Coupe,* for use. He could not afford it, and Mrs. Warin and he had a knock-down-drag-out about the expense, but he reasoned that with it, he could travel faster and farther and serve additional patients. And Mrs. Warin could travel to church in style. Of course, too many of his patients couldn't pay using cash, but did so with chickens and produce. He didn't bring that up to his wife. The day's early summer weather was perfect, so he readied himself and the car, and decided to visit Clara Allerton first. The injection eased his pain, and he thought the poor young woman shouldn't need to wait until later for her relief. He maneuvered the auto onto the road.

Clara was suffering. The three pregnancies which had resulted in three dead babies and one live one had sapped her strength and destabilized her psyche. The living twin boy, Tomas, was as lively as he could be, but she had little energy to chase after him. The third delivery damaged her physical body, and she was rarely without twinges and throbbings even though it was almost two years ago. She knew she disappointed her husband continually by refusing him the ease of her body, but the pain was insufferable, and the doctor had warned her and her husband that additional pregnancies could very well prove disastrous. When Doctor Warin offered the small bottle of laudanum to Clara and explained its use, she was fearful at first, but then became grateful.

"Five or six drops mixed with water should ease your pain and get you through the worst of it," he explained to her, "The taste is bitter, but you can always mask it with a bit of honey."

Clara did find the taste bitter. The honey helped. But the comfort and relief obtained from the drink so improved her life and outlook that if only six drops helped, ten must be better. It was. And then eleven and twelve allowed her to play with Tomas and get some of the household tasks done. She found that a small drink in the morning using only five drops or so, would assist in completing the morning tasks, and another small sip in the afternoon would set her up for the remainder of the day. The small bottle had not lasted the entire month, so during the following visit with the doctor, Clara explained that the bottle must not have had as many drops as the doctor thought and could, perhaps, two bottles be assigned to get her through the month? Doctor Warin understood and agreed, and now Clara needed additional drops to get through the day and sleep at night. She had used up the two bottles and had been without any of the miracle remedy for a few days and was suffering.

She knew the doctor would be coming soon. She planned to ask him about the itching on her back. Her husband had looked and said he saw nothing there except for her scratch marks. They searched the bedding for bugs, but none were found. Then there was the dryness of her mouth. Her teeth felt fine. Nothing needed pulling, but she was always in need of a sip of water or tea, and her tongue felt almost too large. These were minor concerns, however, compared to the absence of the tincture. And when Clara heard an automobile and her husband shout "Hello" to the driver, she sighed with deep relief.

She bent down to gather Tomas into her arms and went out to the porch to wait. Her husband and the doctor were speaking. Clara waited impatiently until the doctor waved good-bye, and the man went back into the woodshop. The automobile eased up to the front of the house, and Clara managed a smile as the doctor stopped the machine, got down, took off his duster and goggles, and lifted his bag to take into the house. He walked up the stairs and chucked Tomas under his chin as the child turned his head, hiding his face on Clara's shoulder.

"Good morning, Clara. What a fine-looking young boy. Let's go inside so I can check him out. Lovely day, isn't it?"

Clara smiled and nodded, and the three of them went inside. The doctor placed his bag on the kitchen table and sat down on a chair.

"Doctor Warin," began Clara, still holding Tomas, "would you like a cup of coffee?"

"Maybe later. Let me see this child of yours." He stood up, and from his vest pocket, he removed two animal crackers and held them out to Tomas who immediately left his mother's arms and reached for them. "Always works," laughed the doctor who set the child on the table and proceeded to examine him.

"Seems healthy and hearty, Clara. Teeth coming in fine, and bones are strong. Feet are well-formed as are the legs. I'm guessing this one keeps you running," and the doctor finished checking the boy's ears as he chewed at the crackers. "And how are you feeling? Is your strength coming back? You look a bit thinner since last month. I hope you are eating enough and drinking plenty of liquids."

Clara nodded. "I'm fine except for a couple things," and explained about the dryness and itching.

"Hmm. Let me see your throat," and Doctor Warin gave her the same examination he had just completed on her son. "No redness. Let's check the ears and heart," and he completed the exam. "Heart is beating a bit quickly, but I see nothing wrong with your skin or anything else. Clara. Try drinking more water or tea, and make sure you eat a hearty dinner," and the doctor looked speculatively at her. "Do you have any of those drops left?"

Clara shook her head and then added as a lie, "I reached over to get something from the side table and accidently knocked over and spilled the last bottle. So clumsy. I will take more if you have it, and I'll be careful this month."

Doctor Warin nodded and pulled out a larger bottle from his bag. "Well, you seem a little run down, so this should keep you for the month. Just watch your dosage. You aren't overdoing it, are you?'

"No, Sir. And thank you. Would you like that coffee now?" Clara brightened up when she saw the larger bottle and gave her savior a smile.

"Think not, but thanks. I need to get to my other patients. Now, drink plenty of water and eat, Clara. This child of yours will keep you busy, and you seem fit although slight. You need to keep your strength up. Come on, child," and he lifted Tomas down from the table who immediately ran over to the dog to offer her the remainder of the animal cracker he had munched.

Clara walked the doctor out, and they spoke of minor things, modest thoughts, as they stood for a time on the porch. Then the doctor, dressing in his driving togs, climbed into his vehicle, and waved as he drove away. Clara waited until he turned on the main road and then hurried back inside. Tomas and the dog were playing and since they were occupied, she mixed her honey water and judiciously measured eight drops from the larger bottle Dr. Warin left for her. She drank the concoction down thinking how beneficial this medicine had proven to be. It helped her to deal with her duties on the farm and her husband and the child and the sadness and pain of it all. The eight drops should suffice for now. She could take more later.

***

For a week or so, Clara felt well. At least, better. She was careful in her use of the drops, drank more water and tea, and ate a second helping at supper even though she did not want it. She was given some rose water from her sister, Jennifer, and it seemed to help alleviate the skin itchiness. A daily walk with Tomas was instituted, and the weather cooperated. She and her husband were getting along. One night, they revisited the passion they enjoyed when they first married, when it was just the two of them, when the ghosts of children did not insist upon taking up the space between them, keeping them apart.

Contentment did not last. The summer weather became mountingly uncomfortable, and the rose water was no longer helping the itchiness of Clara's skin. Tomas fussed and cried because incoming teeth were bothering him, and he was troubled by the heat and the increased inattention of his mother. Arguments between Clara and her husband were amplified. He didn't understand why Clara couldn't get the breakfast dishes done by supper time or care for the truck patch which needed weeding or mend the pants he asked her to weeks ago. What did she do all day while he was working in the miserably hot woodshop making cabinets and boxes and filling the orders which would help to support them? Then the terrible wracking pain that came monthly rendered Clara immobile. Part of her was overwhelmingly thankful that no new life had started, but she could barely stand to make breakfast, and picking up Tomas became impossible. The only amelioration she had were the drops given to her by Doctor Warin, and she no longer limited herself to the eight or ten, but the water turned a dark reddish-brown color as additional drops were added.

It was the last Wednesday of late August. The weather had been overcast and humid all week, and the heat extracted every bit of energy from Clara. Fifteen drops in water allowed her to sleep. Ten drops in the morning worked for getting her up to feed Tomas and make breakfast. Placing an additional six or eight drops in the mid-morning tea helped drive her through until lunchtime. The afternoon nap both she and Tomas claimed was assisted by a sip of water with another five drops. Adding honey to the drink was no longer necessary because she was no longer concerned about the taste. She had become used to the bitterness which heralded relief. She even welcomed it.

That morning, she and her husband fought again. The laundry was not done, the house needed sweeping, Tomas had not been bathed, and he was beginning to smell. What was wrong with her? Clara just stood and stared at her husband, not responding, or reacting or acknowledging, and finally he left, pushing the kitchen chair over in his frustration, and startling Tomas who began to cry. Clara stood still and then went to her son and picked him up. He did smell. She was failing as a wife, a housekeeper, and now a mother.

Although her movements were slow and deliberate, she managed to spend some time washing Tomas and finding clean clothes for him. She kissed him and placed him on the rag rug to play with the small wooden animals his father had carved for him. He was clean and content and moved the sheep and goat and horse out of their carved keepsake box. While he played, Clara swept the floor around him and washed the dishes. She went to the bedroom and combed through her hair, piling it neatly on top of her aching head. She had taken quite a few drops already this morning, but she was exhausted by activity and thought more would help. A glass of water held fifteen drops and she swallowed it quickly. A sudden discomfort in her lower extremities reminded her that her monthly pain continued, and she thought additional drops would help to ease them, so she added more to another glass of water and didn't bother counting them. She swallowed the bitterness.

Clara felt woozy and went out to the kitchen where Tomas was setting up the pig and chickens next to the other animals. "Mama," he called and pointed to his creation, but she disregarded him. Clara went over to the kitchen chair her husband had knocked down, placed it upright, and sat in it facing Tomas. She watched her son play but was growing tired. Her eyes had trouble staying open, and her thoughts didn't seem to make sense. Once she noticed another young boy next to Tomas and tried to discern who he was. He looked familiar. *Oh*, she thought, *it's Edward, Tomas's brother. They are playing together.* She watched as they continued to play. Her eyelids grew heavier; she felt a darkness and a coldness enter her. *The cool feels good in this heat. It comforts me*, she thought. She was having trouble completing sentences in her mind, so she stopped. Her arm dropped down to her side and her cooling body sunk a little in the chair, and as Tomas continued playing with his wooden animals, Clara's heart slowed, and her head fell to one side, and the heat in the newly-swept kitchen no longer troubled her.

***

Time passed. In the woodshop, Clara's husband decided he was hungry. He was also feeling guilty for his actions at breakfast and decided to go in and make amends with his wife. She had seemed overwhelmed lately, and perhaps when Doctor Warin came for his monthly visit in a week or so, he would talk to him and ask if there was something that would help Clara, some treatment, a medication, an elixir. Maybe she needed additional help. The farm work might be too challenging with a child to care for. Perhaps they could afford to hire one of the young neighboring farmgirls to help with the chores. He would talk to Clara about this, and next week, he would inquire about some help. He wasn't the easiest person to live with. He knew this. He had become withdrawn and remote, and the past two years of marriage were taxing. He took off his carpenter's apron and stretched his back and walked towards the house. As he entered, he could hear his son chattering.

Tomas was on the rug surrounded by his wooden animals. The dishes were done, but no lunch was made, and Clara was in a kitchen chair. Tomas saw his father come in, and he smiled and pointed to Clara and said, "Mama sleep," and then got up and toddled over to him. His father bent down to pick him up, looking closely at his wife. She was slumped in the chair with one arm hanging down and the other leaned across her chest. One eye was completely closed and the other was partly open, and out of her slack mouth a dribble of brownish-red liquid clung to her cheek, and a stain of the wetness could be found on Clara's dress.

Her husband had helped to lift enough bodies into the caskets he created to know what Clara had become. He put Tomas down and walked over to Clara to ascertain the truth of the matter. There was no breath, no movement, no life. He put his arms under her, picked up her frail and still soft body, and went to the bedroom to lay her on the bed. He could not show emotion yet. His small son was calling for him.

He went to the kitchen and picked up Tomas. "Mama is sleeping. Let's take a ride to your Aunt Jennifer's house and leave her sleep," he told Clara's son. They walked out to the barn, and Tomas was placed into the wagon while his father harnessed the horse and got in beside him.

"Mama?" asked the boy.

"Mama is sleeping," his father answered. He clicked his tongue saying "Git, now" to the horse, and they began to move.

Chapter 11   1923-1925

Belle refused to marry me.

"Tom, *mon amour*, why? Because of the baby? It's not necessary. I don't care what people think or say. I'll be a wonderful mother, and you'll be the grandest father, and it will be fine. What do you care about gossip?"

"Belle, I'm thinking about the child and you. Where are you going to live now? Not the boarding house. As soon as you are noticed, you'll be asked to leave. If we marry, I can give the baby a name, and we can find a place to live together."

"The child will have a name. She will be *Blanche* after my mother, or he will be *Louis* after my father, and Mama will stop being angry with me and delighted with a grandchild. We can live together. Why not? No one needs to know about us. We will be the perfect family and live together in joy," and then she kissed me and made me dance around until I quit talking about it.

I could not convince her. She said marriages turn out badly, and all we needed to do was to look around. She said even her parents' marriage was filled with problems. Her father, now dead, had repressively ruled their household, and she and her sister, Bertha, would hear the shouting and crying a marriage brings. She said I would start to *own* her and make her unhappy. She claimed true love needed no paper certificate. She was positive we would be happier just being together, and that I should start to look for a small house or apartment. She ran her hands over her small rounded belly and agreed she would need to leave the boarding house soon.

It wasn't having a child without being married that bothered me. Truthfully, it didn't bother me that much. I was panicked about the birth. I hadn't told Belle about my marriage to Ava, or about my son, and his death. I couldn't. I was frightened and more than nervous. I wanted Belle to quit work. She was due to have the baby around the start of the new year, and it was now August. It was hot and humid, and all I could think of was Ava and how she suffered in this heat. I knew what a factory was like in the heat. I worked in one. Every time Belle left for her job, I worried until I saw her and made every effort to see her nightly. I worried about her walking to work, about not being careful around traffic. I worried about her taking chances as she skipped along the sidewalk, laughing with her friends. I worried about her not eating enough or not eating properly. I worried that the nights I could not see her, she would go out and dance and smoke even though she promised she would not. I worried about the drinking. I worried constantly, and spent my free time being with her or looking for a place for us to live. Then I found something.

There were three steps down to a small one-bedroom garden apartment in a building called the *Louis Apartments*. Belle said it was a sign of good luck for the baby who, if a boy, would have that name. I feared having another son. I thought that a boy might be weak. I thought of my three dead brothers and my dead son. Perhaps a girl would be stronger, would be able to survive the trip into this world. I said nothing to Belle and assured her that I was delighted and would welcome either a son or a daughter. Belle agreed it didn't matter and talked about the names again.

"A girl would be called *Blanche Joanna*, and a boy would be *Louis Thomas*, after you, *n`est-ce pas?"*

I smiled a sad smile and brushed the hair that had fallen into her face back. I couldn't have a son named after me again.

"Perhaps *Louis Edward*, after my twin brother who died. What do you think?"

"Yes, Tom. That will be perfect."

And it was settled.

***

I moved into the small apartment by myself, and told the landlord that my wife was coming from another town and would be with me shortly. I spent the next month cleaning the place and looking for second-hand furniture. I organized the small kitchen, and in the bedroom, I arranged my four books on top of the the used dresser I hauled into the apartment. My tools and a few other things I owned were set into a box in the corner, and my knapsack and bedroll were thrown into the back of a small closet. I felt I was creating a real home. There was a very small outside area just beyond the door, and I looked forward to sitting there in the sun with Belle and our child. I began to plan and to be happy and pushed the thought of past losses out of my mind.

I wanted to make a bed for the baby. I didn't have all the tools necessary to do so, but I spoke to my foreman, John, at work, and explained that my wife and I were expecting our first child, and we needed a bed. I told him we couldn't afford to buy one of the fine childbeds made in the factory and would have to make do with what I was able to create. I wanted it to sound as if I would have preferred to buy a factory-made bed, but I knew I could make a better one, and I did. He allowed me to work there using the factory's tools, if I worked through my lunchbreak, and didn't talk about the project. He was surprised at the workmanship and admired it, and when it was complete, he allowed a factory truck to bring it to the apartment where I set it in the corner of the bedroom. The foreman was a good person, and the fact he had five of his own children, I suspect, had something to do with his generosity.

It was late September, and Belle needed to move out of the boarding house. On a Sunday, when neither of us worked, we moved her clothes and belongings into the apartment. We organized our possessions, putting the soap and towels in the small bathroom, and arranging our second-hand kitchen equipment in the cabinets. We placed the plant Ben and Helen gave us on the side table near the front window and began our life as husband and wife. I was getting used to calling her that, and again, asked if we could make it legal. Again, she refused. But she took the carved heart made of hearts I gave her for Christmas and installed it on a small shelf in the kitchen. "There," she claimed pointing at it, "there is our marriage certificate," and she kissed me. In hindsight, it was better that we didn't marry.

She could only work for another eight weeks or so, and I talked her into telling the story that she secretly married me some time ago, so when she left the factory, it wouldn't be under questionable circumstances. She laughed at me and didn't seem to be upset that we were unmarried and bringing a child into the world. Honestly, I was surprised at myself and my contrived morality. But I knew that the world judged and judged harshly, and it was easier, despite Belle's decided non-conformity, to stay within the boundaries of society. It would be easier for our child.

***

The middle of January was when Louis Edward was born. I used the money I had left from my time in Bonneville with Mrs. Vogel to pay a doctor to attend Belle. Belle was angry at me for insisting upon this, but I couldn't explain to her that I had lost one child and feared losing another. I also feared for her life. I asked around at work about hiring a doctor, but the only information I was given were directions to the one hospital in Stone City, called St. Raphael's Hospital. I traveled there to find a doctor, but the workers were not friendly and kept telling me to leave unless I was sick. I left. But I returned twice more, and finally, a sympathetic nurse gave me the name of a young doctor who worked there. When I finally found and spoke to him, he suggested Belle come into the hospital to have the child, but that cost was much more than I could afford. I talked him into coming to the apartment when she was in labor, and for that I gave him my remaining twenty dollars.

By that time, Belle and her mother had made up, and, just as Belle had predicted, Blanche Garnier was thrilled at the thought of a grandchild. She also assumed we were married, and I cautioned Belle not to tell her otherwise. Blanche stayed with us in our small apartment and helped to care for Belle. I was glad she was there although she was also upset at the thought of a doctor coming to help with the baby. She didn't trust them. She thought that a man helping a woman to give birth was unholy and corrupt, and while she and Belle railed against me regarding this, I did not back down. And when Belle was in labor, the doctor was there, her mother was there, and I was instructed to leave and told not to return for at least one day.

When I did come home, ragged, and tired from work and from walking the cold streets, the doctor was gone. Blanche had just made a hot and hearty stew, Belle was asleep, and Louis Edward was in the small bed I had made for him, looking healthy and sucking on his tiny fist. I was so relieved that I sat at the kitchen table, put my head down, and cried.

"Ah non!" said Belle's mother when she saw me, "You are a Papa, and this is a happy time. Go, wash up and come here. I will feed you, and you can hold little Louis Edward. Go now," and I did as she said.

The child was healthy. I didn't ask what the doctor did, because all I cared about was that Belle was safe and my son was alive. He must have given Belle something to make her sleep. When she woke up, she saw me holding our son, smiled, and held out her arms for him. Blanche stayed with us until spring, and while we were crowded, her presence was comforting, and we were a real family. When it was time for her to return to her own house and Bertha, her other daughter, I walked her there, carrying her suitcase and encouraged her to hold on to my arm for safety's sake. I spoke sincerely to her, thanking her for all her help, and telling her she needed to visit regularly.

"I will, Thomas,' she said once we were at her door. "Take care of Belle and Louis Edward. I know Belle can be a handful, and I only hope motherhood will tame her." I kissed her cheek, thinking she was a much better mother-in-law than Mrs. Turner had been and went home to Belle and my son.

***

We ended up calling the child Eddie. For a long time, Belle and Eddie and I stayed happily together in the small apartment. I worked some extra shifts each week because I now had three people to support. Belle talked about going back to work, but I discouraged that move, and while Eddie was young and needy, she seemed content to stay at home with him. We enjoyed watching our son learn to crawl and then to walk and say his first words. He was healthy and sturdy, and I was glad that my last bit of money from Mrs. Vogel had gone to the doctor who helped him safely enter this world. The first Christmas season was joyous, and while Belle and I could afford no presents, I spend nights after work carving and making wooden toys to place under the tiny tree we decorated for Eddie on Christmas morning. I remembered the carved keepsake box containing the carved animals I had as a child, and I took my time and made one for Eddie.

His loved playing with them, taking them in and out of the box, lining them up on the floor, arranging them in different patterns. We taught him the names of the animals: cat, dog, horse, cow, goat, chicken, and a half dozen more. Belle named them in French: *chat, chien, cheval, vache, chevre, poule,* and I was pleased that my son would grow up knowing two languages.

Eddie's first birthday came, and it was cold and snowy, but I insisted on paying for a taxicab so that Blanche and Bertha, could come and spend the weekend and celebrate with us. Ben and Helen, who had gotten married months before, were there also. It was a grand time. I'm not sure where Ben got it, but he produced some whiskey, and Belle brought out glasses, and we toasted Eddie who soon fell asleep. I watched as Belle drank another glass and then one more, and insisted we all sing. She danced around, her curly hair flying, reminding me of the times in the speakeasies. A small snarl of worry entered my mind, and when I glanced at Blanche watching her daughter, I noted a disturbance in her eyes and a vexation around her mouth. I remembered her hoping *motherhood will tame her,* and Fretfulness entered the room.

The winter was long, and in that small apartment with nothing to do except clean it and play with a child, Belle became restless. She complained that on the days I worked additional hours at the factory, there was nothing for her to do. She was bored. "I have only a one-year-old with me. I miss my friends and the fun we had," she would tell me, "I can't wait until spring so we can get out of here. Do you need to work so many hours? I am lonely here, Tom."

I worked every chance I got, and I know I was away for long hours, but I couldn't tell her why. A decent used Singer sewing machine was available, and I was working extra hours to buy it for her. I needed to save up thirty-eight dollars, and almost had that amount. The man who was selling it said he would hold it for me, and I wanted to surprise her. She had never made anything with the red material I gave her that Christmas, and I wanted to see her in that dress with the sparkly hair clips. I planned to ask Blanche to watch Eddie so Belle and I could have a wonderful dinner and then dance like we used to. Belle continued to be despondent and unhappy. She complained about me working and her being stuck at home. There were no smiles, and I watched as she stared out the small front window at night, watching people walk past our apartment.

Spring came. One day, after work, I came home from the second-hand store pushing a baby stroller. I had spent some of my sewing machine savings on it, and it would cause me to work a few weeks longer, but I thought it was an important purchase. I knew Belle wanted to get out and walk, but with a small baby who would walk and fall, and walk and fall again, there was little chance of getting too far from our apartment. The weather improved, and Belle took Eddie in the stroller for long walks. There were some evenings I would come home and they weren't yet back from their walk, and I would wait outside watching for them, worried about where they were.

One such evening, as I saw Belle round the corner pushing the stroller, I could hear her singing. As she came closer, her face appeared flushed, and when she saw me, she yelled, "Hello, Tom! Look, Eddie. It's Papa!" and she pushed the stroller faster. When she stopped in front of the apartment, I could tell she had been drinking. She twirled around and then curtsied and laughed. She saw that I was upset.

"*Mon amour*, it's a lovely night for dancing, isn't it? Look, Eddie, your Mama can dance!" and she spun around again. Eddie looked at Belle, turned to me, began to cry, and lifted his hands to be taken out of the stroller. I reached down and took him out, and realized that he was dirty and smelly. His diaper needed changing, and he cried harder and clung to me.

"Let's get into the apartment, Belle. It's late and Eddie needs to be cleaned up. When was the last time you fed him?" I was angry and disturbed but did not want to make a scene outside when people were walking around, watching us. I held Eddie with one arm and the stroller with the other and stepped down the three steps and opened the door. Belle followed me, and I could tell that there was going to be an argument. We rarely argued, but the few times we had, I always gave in to whatever she wanted. I tried to make her happy because most of the time, she made me happy, but this was different. This wasn't just about something I wanted or she wanted. This time, Eddie was involved.

When she came into the apartment, she sat in the chair in the small living room, and watched me take care of Eddie. I cleaned him up and and got some milk for him. I heated some broth and cut the crust from some bread, soaked it in the broth, and began to feed him. I didn't look at Belle or say anything to her. She said nothing but just watched. I needed to take care of Eddie and get him to bed before I spoke with Belle.

Once Eddie was fed and he began to yawn, I took him into the bedroom we all shared and got him to sleep, placing his favorite wooden carved dog we named *Molly* into his arms. I came out to deal with Belle, but she had fallen asleep in the chair. I stood looking at her for a while. She had on her trousers and a blouse that was not meant for wearing out during the day. Her curly hair had been pulled back and tied with with the red ribbon she favored, but it had come loose, and the ribbon had fallen on the floor beside her. One of her shoes had come off. I let her sleep and put one of the blankets from our bed over her. As quietly as possible, I made myself something to eat, cleaned up, and making sure the door was locked, I turned out the lights and went to bed.

The following morning, I could hear Belle singing quietly to Eddie in the kitchen, so I got up and got ready for work. When I walked out, Belle was still dressed in the clothes from yesterday, and she looked at me sheepishly. "Look, Eddie, It's Papa. Will he yell at Mama? Let's find out."

I didn't want to argue, and I didn't have time. "Belle, I'm just worried. You took Eddie out and didn't care for him, and you had been drinking. Where were you?"

"I found some of my old friends. There was a small party at someone's apartment, and Eddie and I went. I am bored here, Tom. It was a nice day and a fun time, and someone had some made some gin, and it had been soooo long since I had any. I just needed to get out for a while."

There was no time to argue. I looked at her and sighed. "Please, Belle, don't do that again. Eddie needs you to watch him. Please."

She looked at me and didn't say anything. She just sat there, and I didn't have time for additional conversation. "I need to get to work. I'll see you both tonight. I'm not working late," and I bent over to kiss Eddie and left.

I was almost at work when I realized that I hadn't kissed Belle good-bye. She hadn't kissed me either.

***

Belle stayed at home for the next month, and then it happened again. This time, once I got Eddie cleaned and fed and to bed, I didn't let the incident go. Belle and I had the loudest fight possible in whispers. We didn't want to wake Eddie. I told her she was not to take Eddie out with her and go drinking again. She said I was not her husband and this was exactly why she didn't want to be married. I warned her that whoever these friends were, they were not true friends. She answered that she needed to have some fun, and these friends loved Eddie, and he was safe with her. I said she was a mother and had responsibilities. She said something in French to me, and again, I could not translate it, but the meaning was clear. Then she went into the bedroom, shutting the door so as to not wake Eddie, and I tried to make myself comfortable sleeping on the floor in the living room that night.

There were additional times and more fights, and I never knew if she and Eddie would be home when I got there. During the rest of the summer and through the fall, a wall developed between us. Only Eddie made us happy and kept us together. I demanded to know who these friends were, but Belle said there were different ones, and she visited them at different apartments, and I should stop trying to control her. She could do as she pleased, and she would take Eddie with her because the friends all liked him, and he was safe, and she was happy and had a good time, and on and on. And then one day, I came home and the woman from upstairs was waiting for me. She had Eddie on her lap, and he was sobbing.

"Belle asked me to watch your son. She said she had an errand to run and would be back in an hour. That was before noon today, and it is after six now. Really, Thomas, I don't mind watching him for her, but this is the latest she has been gone."

It was then I realized Belle had been going out during the day and leaving Eddie. I was furious. I thanked the woman and took Eddie in and cleaned and fed him and put him to bed. I waited for Belle. This had to stop. I couldn't allow her to put our son in danger or to just leave him like she did. I waited up until midnight, falling asleep in the chair. Belle never came home.

The next morning, I gathered Eddie's things, and took him to Blanche. I didn't know where else to go with him, and I had no idea where Belle was. I explained things to Blanche and got to work late and was docked an hour's pay. I could barely keep my mind on my job, and when I got to Blanche's, to pick up Eddie, she had not heard from Belle. That night, I left Eddie with his grandmother and went back to the apartment alone. Belle was there, and this time, the fight was not staged in whispers.

***

Winter came, and the cold weather kept Belle home. Most of the time. There were a few times I had to collect Eddie from the upstairs woman, Mrs. Kelly, who looked pityingly at me and sighed. There were other times I had to take Eddie to Blanche and was docked an hour's pay again. There were many fights, and on some nights when I came home, Belle was there, but the house smelled like cigarettes, and she smelled like gin, and I knew her friends had just left. I didn't know what to do, so I did nothing.

Another Christmas came. I gave Belle the Singer sewing machine, hoping to make her happy, hoping to improve our relationship. She smiled and thanked me, and hugged me for the first time in a long while, but she never used the machine. It remained in the corner of the bedroom until the day I had to sell it. The new year arrived, and soon after, Eddie turned two-years-old. A birthday party was held, and there was a birthday cake for him, but only his grandma, Blanche, came to celebrate with us. Eddie was the joy of my life. Whenever he saw me, he would say, "Papa!" and come running to me with his arms outstretched. I would pick him up and twirl him around, and he would laugh and say, "Again, again," and he would kiss my cheek.

Belle and I exchanged no kisses. Sometimes she was home, and other times she was gone. Sometimes Eddie was with her; sometimes he was left with Mrs. Kelly upstairs; sometimes he stayed with his grandmother, Blanche. The year passed, and things did not improve. There were fights, and we yelled and no longer worried about whispering, and Eddie cried when he heard the arguments. Belle's prediction that we would *be a perfect family and live in joy* did not happen, and the situation became desperate.

Chapter 12   1901

Clara's mother and sister, Jennifer, were by her bedside trying to comfort the eighteen-year-old as she squirmed and cried and moaned through her second day of labor. They had sent the husband to town to see if Doctor Warin was available to come and assist with, what they knew from their own experiences, was not a normal birth, but he had not returned yet. They took turns calming and reassuring Clara and stoking the fire in the stoves attempting to keep the chill of the late January wind and ice from entering the bedroom. Clara alternated between throwing off the quilt and blanket and demanding additional coverage. The women attending her watched her agony, listened to her whimpers, and fidgeted with remembered pain.

"Where is he? Is the doctor coming? Mother!"

"I'm here, Clara. He's not here yet, but will be soon. Would you like your back rubbed some more? Perhaps you should get up and walk around for a while again," and her mother pushed back her daughter's dark hair which was sweaty and smelled of vomit because part of it wandered into the bucket which Clara had used to rid herself of partially digested food.

Jennifer who had been looking out the front door, came into the bedroom to say, "Clara, your husband is returning. I see the wagon down the road."

"Is the doctor with him?" hoped the mother.

"I'm not sure. Can't see yet." Jennifer knew he was alone, but did not want to deliver that wretched news. "I'll wait at the front door for him."

Shortly, the door opened and a vestige of cold air entered with the husband whose sunken eyes and forlorn face expressed his failed mission as he closed the the door behind him.

He shoved off his coat and hat and looked at his sister-in-law and knew what she wanted. "The doctor is at the Henderson's, and I left a message with his wife. She said he would be here as soon as he returned, but she wasn't sure when that would be. How is Clara?"

Upon hearing her husband's voice, Clara yelled out for him, and he entered the room where just a year ago they had first engaged in the business of ignoring the night's wintery cold. He was shocked by his young wife's appearance and frightened by the bloody rags which filled one of the porcelain enameled wash pans they had received as a wedding gift. This pain was unfamiliar to him, and he didn't know how to confront it, how to negotiate the agitations it accorded him. He went to the side of his wife, and she clutched his hand and tears ran down her cheeks.

"Is the doctor coming?"

"Soon, Clara, soon."

Clara produced a twisting motion, gave a sudden loud moan, and yelled, "Mother, I have an awful pushing need! What should I do?'

The mother moved the husband away and said, "Time to get this baby out, Clara," and she turned to Jennifer, gave some instructions, and told the husband to, "Wait out there."

He did. Faced with the dreadful sounds from the bedroom, he put his coat and hat and scarf back on and left to tend to the horse and wagon which did not take as long as he wished it would. He went to the chicken coop to check things out and looked towards the woodshop where he thought he could spend some time, but feared being so far away from the significance inside the house. He walked quickly up and down the path to the road many times, but could still hear noises. He went to the chicken coop again and watched the chickens huddle together to keep warm. He repeated travelling the path, and each time he returned to the house, he listened for the wails and shrieks, and when they seemed to quiet down, he walked back to the door, put his ear against it, and listened. Indistinct utterances were detected, so he went in.

His outerwear was removed. There was a quiet sobbing going on in the bedroom, and he went towards the sound thinking it utterances of relief. No baby cried, and he wondered about it. When he got up enough nerve, he pushed open the bedroom door and saw Jennifer bending down to wipe up an unspeakable mess of human muck while the mother stood next to the bed whispering softness to her sobbing daughter who held a wrapped and silent parcel. When Clara saw him, she sobbed louder and said, "Your son, come and hold him," and offered the quietness to him.

He walked over and held out his arms readying his mouth for a smile, but the bundle was still and soundless, and when it was placed into his arms, he thought that perhaps they had made a mistake and had just given him some old wrappings. He looked down into the blue face of a diminutive deadness which did not look like anything else he had ever seen. Perhaps that once, when he was young and walked through the woods and stumbled on a young possum that was left, by an uncaring mother, to rot in a pile of leaves. He felt the package's weight, and eyed the length, and didn't know what to do with it, so the mother took it from him to place back into Clara's arms and murmured she should mourn and remember, should savor her sorrow which would make the next arrival sweeter. But Clara continued to keen and cry, and the women crowded around her, pushing her husband away because his sorrow could not possibly match hers.

He wandered to the kitchen and sat down by the stove not knowing what else to do. His hands came up to his head, one on either side, pushing in, pressing against his brain, attempting to ease out the suffering, the torment. After some time, as the sobbing decreased and then stopped, Jennifer came out to the kitchen carrying the red rags she would dispose of by burning. She regarded him. After placing the scraps in the corner and covering them, she washed her hands and busied herself by making tea. She placed a cup on the table and sat down in a chair across from him.

"The baby needs burial, but the ground is too hard right now at the cemetery."

The hands came down, and he looked at Jennifer and shook his freed head. "He will be buried here in the family gravesite where my father and mother and grandma and Pa are. He'll stay here close to his home. I know what to do. I can pile some dried corncobs and wood on top of the space needed and melt through the frost so I can dig. I'll only need to go down four or five feet. Do you think Clara's father will help?"

Jennifer nodded her head. "Probably, but let me ask my husband. David can come tomorrow morning. Clara is asleep, and the baby is wrapped, and Mother is holding him. She'll stay here overnight to make sure Clara is well, but we need to take care of the baby soon. If you can take me home in a few hours, I'd appreciate it. I need to clean up. I'll be back with David tomorrow and stay with Clara so Mother can go."

He nodded his head and said, "That's fine. Give me a couple of hours in the woodshop. I'll be back then," and leaving the untouched cup of tea on the table, he shrugged on his coat, took his hat, and went out the door.

When he got to the shop, he started the stove to warm the place up and walked to the back to examine the wood piled there. In the storage area he found some maple planks and pulled them out. There was not enough to create a casket for an adult, but there was enough to make a small one. One just large enough to cradle a tiny creature, barely larger than a young possum. The entire process wouldn't take too long. A couple of hours would do. He moved the planks to the large workbench in the front of the shop, near the stove, and began to measure.

***

Fifteen months later, when the husband burned the corncobs and wood and dug the second grave close to the first, he envisioned the headstone. This one would have a name chiseled onto it, not simply a designation and date: *Son, 1901*. Clara insisted on naming the second baby *Edward* which happened to be both her father's and his father's name, so he readily agreed. *Edward, 1902* would appear on the new headstone. For this birth, Doctor Warin was present, although it can't be said that he had much to do with the birthing process other than to stand by and guide Jennifer and Clara's mother with unneeded and unwanted advice.

Edward survived the difficult labor. He was smallish and delicate, weighing barely as much as the five-pound bag of potatoes, and there was great fear when he had difficulty suckling, but eventually he caught on. He might have lived longer than a month had it not been for that persistent cough and the wheezing which appeared in the first week of birth and never went away despite the drops of Mrs. Winslow's Soothing Syrup the doctor recommended. "One drop should suffice," he instructed, "but not more than that. As he gets older, perhaps two will be needed."

March was the birth month, and the weather remained cold and windy, but Clara thought once the spring came and the sun warmed the earth, the cough would dry up. It never did. Early one morning in April when Clara woke, her first thought was that the two drops given had allowed baby Edward to sleep through the night. No coughing was heard. No wheezing was noticed. No breathing of any kind was present, and the lamenting and wailing continued for days.

This second sacrifice affected both parents severely. Clara refused to have Edward removed from her arms for most of that day. She alternately sobbed and sang to him, attempting to get the cold, blue babe to take the breast, her milk dripping down her front, moistening her dress, wetting her shawl, falling onto her shoe. Finally, her physical fragility gave way to acquiescence, and she submitted to her sister's quiet convincing. Jennifer took the child as Clara's mother held her daughter, murmuring gentleness and tenderness into her ears, wiping away her own tears, alarm for Clara's frame of mind seeping into her thoughts.

Clara refused to go to the family burial site and watch as her husband placed Edward's expertly and swiftly made casket four and a half feet into the ground where the burning corncobs had softened the still frosted soil and allowed for digging. Jennifer stayed with her sister and held her as she sobbed herself to sleep, cabbage leaves bound to her breasts to help the healing, a few drops of Mrs. Winslow's Soothing Syrup stirred into the chamomile tea Clara was encouraged to drink.

Later that day, when the husband came into the house, he sat in the chair close to the stove and allowed Molly, the dog, to comfort him by laying across his muddied boots. Never a talkative man, the husband drew into himself like the reclusive, solitary, muted, mud turtle which dwelled in the pond where, years ago, he used to fish with his grandfather.

***

Sorrow filled the farm for months. Clara and her husband barely spoke to each other, and the silence generated a facsimile of winter through the spring and summer and warm autumn months. As genuine winter approached, they eased the fencing between them and began to speak of the future. They chose to ignore the past, and perhaps this was beneficial to the marriage, for they again shared a bed and comforted each other in the wintery dark.

When, after the first of the year, Clara determined that another miracle was due in the early fall, she fell into a deep despondency. Her husband would find her sitting at the kitchen table, the winter apples she was peeling turned brown in the bowl because she forgot her task while staring into vagueness. She wouldn't go to Sunday services to face either the consolatory gazes or the congratulatory comments of the congregation. She permitted no discussion of gender or names with her sister or mother, and the infant particulars she had locked away from the previous ventures remained locked away in the solid red cedar chest her husband had constructed and carved with her initials for a wedding gift. She was silent on the matter, and only during the warm summer nights when she could not sleep and sat on the porch in the rocking chair, did she rub her belly and wonder and hope. For his part, her husband was hushed and put anticipation aside. Without her knowledge, he had manufactured an additional small wooden coffer which he hid behind the large planks of pine and white oak and which he yearned to never need.

The bad news was, it was needed. The good news was, it wasn't. Clara gave birth to twin boys. The second child did not live. He was spit out behind his older brother, and a cord kept him from life. He was named Edward and buried in the small casket his father had hidden behind the large planks of pine and white oak. His brother, the first-born, appeared and let a strong, healthy yell out as the doctor held him. While his dead brother was cleaned and wrapped and set to the side until he could be further dealt with, the brother who cried was placed into the arms of his exhausted mother. His father came next to the bed and watched and felt the tightening in his gut and heart loosed. He touched the soft and healthily flushed cheek of his son and named him *Tomas*.

Chapter 13   1926-1927

Belle left the apartment. Because I had to work, and she wasn't there to take care of Eddie, I had to find someone who would. I paid our upstairs neighbor, Mrs. Kelly, to watch him Monday, Tuesday, and Wednesday, since those were the days she didn't work at a restaurant. Although it was far from the apartment, I took Eddie to be with his grandmother, Blanche, on Thursday and Friday and those Saturdays I worked. Periodically Belle went there to see Eddie, and I was glad for Eddie's sake. Sometimes Belle would bring Eddie back to the apartment on Friday, and would stay overnight. I never knew when she would show up, and I had no idea where she stayed the rest of the time. I told her she couldn't drink when she was with Eddie or at the apartment, and most of the time she didn't.

When Belle was at the apartment, we tried to get along and not fight. I attempted to talk to her, to find out what we could do to settle things between us, but she refused, and for the next year or so, we lived that way. When she was gone, I know she drank and partied and lived a wild life. I heard rumors about her from Ben and Helen who remained my friends and who sympathized with me. Helen especially felt it was her fault.

"I am so sorry, Thomas, for introducing the two of you. There were other girls at the boarding house, and I should have been more aware of Belle's wildness, but you were so lonely, and she seemed so much fun…" and she sighed and shook her head.

"Helen," I assured her, "it's not your fault. You and Ben are good friends. I know you wanted me to be happy, and I was for a while. What Belle does and how she lives her life is her choice, not your fault." I didn't want Helen to worry. She and Ben were expecting their own child soon, and she didn't need to feel distressed about a situation she hadn't caused.

Christmas that year seemed forced although I tried to make it fun for Eddie as the two of us decorated the apartment with a small tree. I invited Ben and Helen for Christmas Eve, but Belle wasn't there. She showed up early Christmas morning when Eddie was still asleep, but it was obvious she had been drinking. She was loud and spiteful, telling me I kept her from her son. I sent her away because she couldn't come in while she was drunk. She turned and swished away, almost falling in the snow, and I watched her get into an automobile with some people I didn't recognize. I closed the door, watched them pull away, laughing, and hoped that Eddie hadn't heard the turmoil.

Eddie's third birthday came in the middle of January, and she showed up again, but was sober and subdued. I let her in. She had brought him an armful of toys. I don't know where she got the money to buy them, and frankly, didn't want to know. She was kind and loving to Eddie who was happy to see her. Ben and Helen were there, and she was polite and talkative to them and held their new daughter and told them how lovely the baby was. She was reasonable and mannerly.

Once Eddie went to bed, and Ben and Helen left with their daughter, Belle stayed to talk. She asked if she could live in the apartment and watch Eddie. I told her Eddie was her son too, but I couldn't trust her, and was afraid for his safety. We spoke civilly for a long time. She left, assuring me she was going to change. She had asked her mother if she could stay there, and on Thursdays and Fridays, she would be with Eddie and prove to me she was reformed. I told her I would consider it, and would see how she acted. Through the rest of the winter, that is what happened. She settled down, and I don't think she was drinking although I didn't know for sure.

In late spring, she moved back into the apartment. I shouldn't have allowed that to happen, but I was eager for things to work out. I thanked Mrs. Kelly for her help, and she looked at me and said, "I hope it works out for you two, Thomas, I really do." I did too.

Sometimes I would come home from work and see Belle and Eddie out in front of the building. Eddie was a three-year-old who ran everywhere just for the pleasure of moving. I jokingly told him that he would win a race one day, and he said, "OK, Papa, I will," and I rumpled his head of dark curly hair, so much like his mother's. He had her spirit too, and when he saw me coming down the street, he would take off and run towards me, his arms open, calling "Papa, Papa," and I would lift him up and twirl around, and we would walk back to the apartment hand in hand.

Things changed. One Friday night, I came home and saw Eddie outside waiting for me. He ran to me as usual, but when we walked back towards the apartment, Belle was not there. She was inside asleep in the chair, and I smelled gin although I did not see a bottle or glass. Eddie had opened the front door and let himself out. I was sick when I pictured what might have happened to him, and I was not gentle when I woke Belle up by shaking her.

"Belle! Wake up! Now!" and she slowly opened her eyes and looked at me. "Do you know where Eddie was? You have been drinking. I can smell it," and I turned away to find Eddie. I was furious and she knew it.

She sat up, got up slowly, and ran to the bathroom quickly. I heard her being sick and decided that Eddie and I needed to leave.

"Come on, Eddie, let's have some fun. We're going to visit Mrs. Kelly at her restaurant and eat supper there. Doesn't that sound great?"

Eddie jumped up and down and clapped. "Mama is coming?"

I didn't hear any sounds from the bathroom except for the water running, and I told him, "Just you and me tonight. This will be our special supper. Let's go," and we left Belle to her sickness.

Belle was remorseful and repentant. She said she had just a small drink from a bottle she found in a cabinet, and it made her sick. It must have gone bad. She would not drink again. She promised, and for some time, she kept her word. But I knew it wouldn't last. I knew Belle.

Summer came with heat. I worked extra shifts and saved up to purchase an Emerson table fan to help cool the apartment. It helped, but sometimes, on the miserably humid nights, the three of us took our blankets outside to the small space we had and tried to make ourselves comfortable enough to get some sleep. One exceedingly warm night, we organized our blankets and Eddie snuggled between us, happy to be there. Soon he fell asleep, and Belle and I stayed awake. We whispered back and forth over Eddie's dark curly head of hair.

"You know, Thomas, I never thought we would come to this. I really thought we would have a great life."

"I know, Belle. I hoped we would."

She was silent for a time. Then she whispered, "I wonder, if I had agreed to marry you, would our life be different? What do you think?"

I couldn't imagine us married now and asked, "Would marriage keep you from drinking?"

"Probably not. I'm sorry Tomas, for being a *mauvaise femme*. I am truly sorry."

I considered what she said. She didn't say she would stop drinking or stay away from those friends, or even that she thought we should marry, which was not something I wanted anyway. She simply apologized for being a *bad woman*. I'm not sure she was. I didn't know what to answer, so I reached over and took her hand and held it as Eddie slept between us. Finally, we slumbered outside, in our small space, with the noise of Stone City around us, and a partial moon above us. It would be the last time the three of us were so familiar, so tranquil, so loving.

***

Belle began to drink and see her friends again. At first, it was only during the evening hours, when I was home and Eddie was safe. She claimed to be going for a walk, but would come back hours later, in the middle of the night, and sleep until I woke her up the next morning. There were a few times she would not wake up, and I hurriedly took Eddie to Blanche's house and chanced being late for work. I couldn't ask Mrs. Kelly upstairs to take him. I was too embarrassed. When I came home with Eddie on those nights, Belle would be serious and low-key and humble. She always had a dinner made and the house was clean, and once Eddie was in bed, she would apologize again and again. And I forgave her again and again.

Then she started to have her friends over during the day. At first, they would be gone by the time I arrived home. But she smelled like the gin they brought with them, and cigarette smoke still hung in the air. We would argue about it.

"I have a right to have friends, Thomas. There are only two of them who were here. You want me to stay at home, but it's still just Eddie and me, and I need some other adults around. I want some fun."

There was little sense in arguing with her. I made the mistake of telling her she was limited to one friend who needed to be gone by the time I arrived home, and Eddie was the top priority and Belle needed to watch after and care for him. I should have put a total stop to it, but part of me held some hope she would change. Part of me feared she would leave again, and part of me wanted her to. It was difficult for all of us. I watched Eddie carefully, wondered how it affected him, how it would harm him. I remembered my own childhood and worried.

It was the last of August, and Labor Day was Monday, September 5. The factory would be closed for three days over that weekend, and it would be a perfect time to go somewhere and do something different. Perhaps the three of us could go to the Stone City Union Station on Jefferson Street and take the train into Chicago. I had never been on a train before and thought Eddie would like it. Maybe Belle would too. I began to ask around about the trip, to see if any of my co-workers had done something similar, to figure out how to go about it. One day, after work, I took a trip to the station to check on the trains and ticket costs and asked the man working in the booth about where to stay once we were in Chicago. He gave me some pamphlets which advertised different hotels and things to see and do, and I was anxious to bring them home and read over them with Belle. I remained hopeful that things could work out between us.

As I walked down our street, I saw an automobile parked on the other side, across from our apartment, and I recognized it. This was the vehicle I had seen Belle get in on those nights she left. These were some of the "friends" I told Belle I didn't want at our house. They had been at the apartment and not left yet, and Belle was standing to the side of the automobile. All of them were laughing loudly, and I could tell from her flushed face and unsteady stance, Belle had been drinking. Eddie was standing to the side watching the group, and I could see him tug on Belle's trousers and hear him crying, "Mama", but she ignored him. As I came closer to the group, Belle turned, saw me across the street, and stopped laughing. Eddie noticed she was looking at something, and he turned to see what it was. When he saw me, he left the group and his mother; he took off and ran towards me; he opened his arms, calling "Papa, Papa"; he wanted me to lift him up and twirl him around and walk back to the apartment hand in hand.

There was no time to yell. He was a fast runner, and I had told him that one day he would win a race. He lost this one. He raced against the automobile that had turned the corner and didn't see, couldn't see the forty-inch child running towards me, running to win the race, running to throw his arms around me, running so he could be picked up and spun around, running so we would walk to the apartment together. This race was Eddie's final one. He would not run again.

***

The cost of the funeral was thirty-nine dollars. I had just paid the rent and had only a few dollars in my pocket. When I went back to the apartment, I looked around the living room and the kitchen. I went to the bedroom and saw the Singer sewing machine I had given Belle for Christmas, the one she had never used. Moving things around the closet, I found the red material, the artificial silk I had given Belle to make that special dress she never made. I searched until I found the flashy hair clips she hadn't worn and gathered all the things together. On my way out, I grabbed the Emerson table fan I worked extra shifts to purchase. I held everything and struggled, but managed to carry it all down the street to the pawn shop where I exchanged everything for thirty-five dollars which I placed into my pocket next to my last seven dollars. When I left, I tore up the tickets which would allow me to buy the items back. I would never need to.

As I opened the door of the funeral parlor, I thought that people in Levett had the right idea. Buy the pine casket from the carpenter, bury it in the family gravesite, pretend to pray. Mr. Overton, the funeral director, watched me come into his office. I counted out the thirty-nine dollars on his desk, then set the additional three down. "Flowers," I barked at him, "As many as possible," and I left.

***

I stayed by myself in the apartment ignoring the heat and the knocks on the door. I waited until late afternoon two days later, then I cleaned up and dressed. I drank some water and ate a piece of stale bread before I left, carrying a box under my arm. I walked into the funeral parlor where people were sitting or standing, and looked around. I didn't know all of them. The ones I didn't know must have been Belle's friends. Belle was there, seated in a chair in the front next to her mother, Blanche, and her sister, Bertha. I noted that Ben and Helen were there, and Mrs. Kelly was seated in the back. John, the foreman from the factory stood in the back holding his cap.

Everyone watched me as I walked up to Eddie. He was wearing new clothes, and someone had placed a rosary in his little hands. I stood there and put my hand on his dark, curly hair and felt the softness. The keepsake box I had brought with me held the carved animals I made for him, and I opened it and took out Eddie's favorite animal, the carved dog named *Molly*. I put the box holding the rest of the animals down the side of the casket, removed the rosary from his hand, putting it down the other side and placed Molly into his hands. I bent down to kiss his cold forehead and whisper into his ear. Then I stood back.

I turned and walked over to Blanche, ignoring Belle, and kissed her. I went to Ben and Helen and hugged them both. Ben pressed a card into my hand, and I placed it in my pocket. Mrs. Kelly watched as I came to her and said "Thank you" and she wiped her eyes. I shook the foreman's hand, thanking him for coming, and he handed me an envelope and said, "From the guys at work." I nodded my acceptance.

I left the parlor and began to walk out the door as I heard my name. It was Belle. She was running after me calling, "Thomas, Thomas!" Tears ran down her face, as she pleaded, "Thomas, please, stay! Please! Let's talk after this. Please!"

I looked at her. She was wearing a dark dress I had never seen, and her hair was neatly pulled back into a knot at the nape of her neck. Her eyes were swollen and red, and she clutched a handkerchief. I hadn't loved her for a long time, but I didn't hate her either. I didn't know what I felt. She reached out to place her hand on my arm, and I removed it. I looked at her and spoke.

"You were right, Belle. You are a *mauvaise femme.*" I turned and went back to the apartment.

***

I opened the door and stood looking around before I moved to the bedroom. My knapsack and old bedroll were in the back of the closet. I took them out and packed for the road, a familiar task. I collected whatever I thought I would need and then remembered the envelopes in my pocket. There was a ten-dollar bill from Ben and Helen, and forty-dollars from the men at the factory. I read the messages, then placed the papers in the trash. I put the money in my pocket. It would help me get to Chicago.

Before I left, I put the key to the apartment on the kitchen counter next to the sink. The rent was paid for the month. Belle would be back. Her clothes were here. She would probably come looking for me. Perhaps I should leave her a note. I looked around for some paper, but then spied the ledge in the kitchen which held the heart made of hearts I had carved for her as a first gift. Our marriage certificate. I took it down and looked carefully at it. It was fine work, and I knew it. I held it for a few minutes, feeling the weight of the wood, running my hands over the small carefully chiseled hearts. I placed it in the middle of the kitchen table and began to search for the tool I knew was in one of the drawers next to the sink. When I found the hammer, I lifted it, and with all the strength I had, brought it down directly into the center of the carved heart which split into pieces. I put the hammer down next to the fragments, picked up my belongings, arranged them on my back, and went out the door.

Chapter 14   1900

Sunday evening, New Year's Eve, 1899, which signified the end of the 1800's, was the wedding date for Clara Hampton and the Allerton boy who lived on the small farm down the road and worked as a carpenter in the woodshop of his deceased grandfather. The farm, the house, the woodshop with all the tools were his, and while he didn't have much in the way of a fortune, Mr. Hampton was happy enough to give the youngest of his four daughters to him in marriage. Clara knew how to cook and keep house, and while she was not yet eighteen, she was happy to be married to this man she had known most of her life. The wedding was small, in keeping with country tradition, and right after midnight, on the New Year's Day of January 1,1900, the married couple left in their wagon and traveled the short distance to the farm.

Clara went into the house, stoked the stove, lit some lamps, and moved into the bedroom. She placed a lamp on the dresser and turned down the bed she would share with her husband that night. Quickly, in the still chilled room, Clara undressed, placing her wedding attire on the rocker in the corner and slipping into her nightdress. She let her hair down and brushed through it, then gathered a shawl to tie around her, but she was still shivery. Unsure whether it was from the winter or her nerves, she opened the cedar chest her husband had made and gifted her for their wedding, and pulled out one of the blankets stored in it to wrap around her shoulders. Feeling comforted, Clara walked to the kitchen, her kitchen, where the stove was beginning to share its warmth. She began to make tea.

Her husband was outside completing chores: putting the horse and wagon away, checking the chickens, wandering around the small homestead, a bit nervous and anxious about going in to his house, his wife, his bed. Their bed. He knew what the night would entail, and was shy about the possibilities and expectations, but it was almost one in the morning, and his chores were done, and he was cold. He walked around the house once more, flapping his arms to keep himself warm, then he walked up the stairs, crossed the porch, opened the door, and, taking a deep breath, went in.

He hung up his coat and hat on the coatrack and took an additional deep breath. The house was beginning to be warm, and he could hear Clara in the kitchen softly humming. When he got to the warmest area, she was standing in the kitchen before the stove, a blanket wrapped around her, making tea. Her long dark hair cascaded against her back, and she looked like a little girl playing house, a scene close to reality. She turned and smiled as her husband came in and said, "I was wondering where you were. Is everything alright? It's awfully cold out there, and I'm making you some hot tea. Come over and warm up."

Her husband stood still for a while against the door, thinking about the last two difficult years. The years after he had buried his grandfather and stayed in this house by himself, waiting for Clara to grow up, to attain the years her father thought she should before becoming a wife. And here she was: his wife. She would ease the loneliness and help with the chores and warm his bed. Suddenly he was not shy, and another, a better feeling, took its place. He walked over to his wife, leaned down to kiss her cheek, took her hand, and disregarding the hot tea, led her into their bedroom. Molly, the dog, had curled up on the bed in her usual place, but the new husband moved her out to the kitchen. When he came back to the bedroom, he smiled at Clara who laughed softly, and they went about the business of ignoring the wintery cold to become what the preacher had called them earlier: man and wife.

The next morning the husband woke up to the warm body beside him and panicked for a second, wondering who it was. Then he remembered. He leaned over to look at his sleeping wife, brushed her hair away from her face, kissed her cheek, and smiled at recollection. He drew on the winter clothes which were laying around the floor and went outside to complete chores quickly. It continued to be frosty and cold. He let the dog outside with him, and Molly walked past, yapping quietly, wondering why she was removed from the bedroom last night, but assumed it was a mistake and would not occur again.

Man and dog came in to the kitchen where the warmth and the smell of coffee greeted them. The dog lapped at her fresh water in the chipped bowl and curled up on top the old blanket next to the protecting stove. The man strode over to his wife and put his arms around her.

"Oh, you're cold!"

"Cold outside. Mmm, the coffee smells good. Maybe we should go back to bed and get warm."

Clara giggled. "Shameful, Husband. I'll make you breakfast and then finish making the pie I need to bake for the dinner at my parents' house today. Everyone will be there to celebrate the new year and new century. Nineteen hundred! Just think, we have lived in two different centuries!"

The husband hugged her again, and then took off his coat, placing it on the back of the kitchen chair into which he lowered himself. He watched his wife prepare his meal, and asked, "Do we need to do that today? Go over to your parents? We could just stay here in front of the fire and stay warm."

She brought him a steaming cup of coffee and placed it in front of him. "Yes, we need to go. This dinner is in part, for us as a celebration, and the neighbors will be there and expect to see us. How do you want your eggs?"

The husband sighed and said, "Over easy is fine. Is there any bread?"

Breakfast was made with the bread which was toasted because it was stale, and the newlyweds sat and ate and got used to being together. Although they had known each other for years, had grown up together, had talked and comforted each other in hard times, there was a particular sort of self-consciousness each felt, due, most likely, to the business of the previous wintery night. After breakfast was completed and the second cup of coffee was slowly sipped, they fell into the coziness married couples share, and matters improved.

Draining the coffee from the cup, the husband commented, "I need to get the wagon out and check on the horse again. Still awfully cold. I'm going to spend an hour or two in the woodshop finishing something. What time should we leave for your parents?'

Clara moved the dishes into the sink. "I told Mother I would help her ready things, so if we leave here by one o'clock, that will be fine. My pie will be done by then. And, I saw a mouse in that corner," and she pointed to the far side of the kitchen, "Isn't there a cat you used to have as a mouser? I think we need one."

"That cat died about a year ago. Just haven't replaced it, but we'll ask around and see if any are available. Think Pa had a trap in the shop, so I'll check for that and set it up in here. Thanks for breakfast, Wife," and he got up to hug her again and whispered in her ear, "If you change your mind about not going, let me know," and Clara giggled again.

***

Later in 1900, when spring was easing out the cold, pushing it back to memory, the husband came home from a delivery trip. One of the farmers out to the south of town had ordered a new bedframe and some wooden crates to replace what had rotted, and the husband completed the task and delivered the items. He pulled up in front of the house and left the wagon to find his wife. She was in the sitting room polishing the rocker and the chairs with a combination of linseed oil and beeswax that her mother had used for years, and she looked up when she heard the door.

"Back already? I'll get some lunch started soon. I'm just about finished here. This rocker needed a good polishing," and she smiled as she continued rubbing the arm with the rag in her hand.

He walked over to her and said, "Better put that down. Don't think you can hold that and these," and out from the inside of his coat, he pulled two kittens, one an orange tabby and the other a calico. "Their cat just had a litter a few months back. Think these will do for mousers?"

Clara put down the soft rag she was using for polishing, and stood up. She held her hands out, and he placed the kittens into her arms. They mewed quietly at her, and she smiled at her husband who grinned back.

"You remembered! Aren't these sweet? Well, this is a surprise, and I guess I have a surprise for you too," and the wife told him her news which involved the consequences of those nights when they went about the business of ignoring the wintery cold.

Chapter 15   1927-1928

Eddie would have liked the Rock Island train ride into Chicago. He would have enjoyed looking out the window and pointing to the passing trees and farm buildings and houses. The train whistle would have, at first, scared him, but after he got used to it, he would have tried to whistle with it, then turned to me and giggled at his noise. The other people in the train would have appreciated his lilting laughter and his three-and-a half-year-old voice saying, "Papa. Look at …the tree, the building, the cow, the house…", and he would have been sitting on my lap, and I would have held onto him carefully, keeping him safe, not allowing him out of my sight. I would have been happy with him, talking and pointing out the various features and answering his questions. Perhaps Belle would have told him the names of the sights in French, and as Eddie grew tired, he would have held tightly to his carved dog, Molly, placed his head back against my chest, his dark eyes shutting in a quick nap, and Belle and I would have looked at him and smiled and then smiled at each other.

But that did not happen on the train ride. I was alone and sad and tired. I decided not to arrive in a strange city late at night, so I spent the time after I left the apartment walking around the darkened Stone City, slowly making my way to the train station, stopping once for a cup of coffee, and again, in the early morning hours, for a breakfast. Then I waited at the station, having purchased my one-way ticket costing fifty-cents, to Chicago. On this journey, I would not walk the fifty or so miles to my destination. I would be deposited in the middle of the town about ten o'clock in the morning, and find my way to a hotel and stay there for a day or two and figure out my next move. I had examined the map of Downtown Chicago, and the streets, and looked at the pamphlet which explained the streetcar system run by the CSL, and where it would go. It was all confusing. There were different neighborhoods, and I knew no one there. And I was glad. Figuring out where I would stay and what job I could get would take all my time and energy, and I wanted that to be the case. I didn't want to think about Eddie. I definitely didn't want to think about Belle.

I slept for a while on the train, and woke up right before we entered the LaSalle Street Station. I gathered my things, left the train, and stood, trying to get my bearings. I needed to ask someone about directions. After a bathroom visit, I noticed the man sitting on a stool behind the ticket office. I got at the end of the line of people and waited my turn.

"Where would you like to go?" the man asked.

"I've just arrived from Stone City. Is there a hotel close around that doesn't cost too much?"

I'm guessing I wasn't the first person to ask this question because he was ready with an answer.

"Try the Wabash YMCA. They usually got some rooms for rent cheap. Here, I'll write down how to get there," and he grabbed a slip of paper and drew a map for me. "Go out that exit," and he pointed, "and follow these directions. Should be about a fifteen-minute walk."

"Thank you, Sir. I appreciate it," and I moved out of the way because a line had formed behind me. I followed the directions, but it took longer to get to there. I stopped and looked up at the tall buildings and around at the different shops and offices. I know I looked like a hayseed, but I didn't care. Chicago was unlike any place I had ever been, and I wanted to take it all in. There were so many people. I wondered where all of them were going. I continued to follow the map to my destination, and when I saw the building, I was relieved. My cash was limited, and I knew I needed to find some work soon.

When I checked in, I had the choice of paying fifty-cents per day with a roommate, or one dollar a day for a single room. While I didn't want to room with a stranger in this strange city, I knew I needed to watch my spending, so I opted for the roommate. For another ten-cents, I could rent a locker where I could secure my things, and I did that. My room was on the sixth floor. I entered an elevator for the first time ever. I got on with three other men, and I was glad because I had no idea how to work the thing. I watched as the men pushed the buttons, and when one pushed the *six*, I was relieved. I got off on that floor and looked for my room number: 624.

I found myself alone in the room, although my roommate's things: newspaper, hat, shaving items, clothes, were around on his bed… the one farthest from the window. I took the one closest to the window and sat on the bed deciding what would go into my security locker and what I would keep out. I counted the money I had and kept about five singles and the change with me while I placed the rest into a pocket and stored the items in the locker. My carving tools and three of my books were locked away. I kept out some clothes and one book and a few personal effects and sat down and stared out the window to think.

I estimated the weekly cost of the room, locker, and a cheap breakfast to be about six dollars per week. I didn't figure in a dinner, and was sure I wouldn't eat a lunch. That would be extra, and I needed to watch my cash until I got a job. I would give myself four or five days here before I moved on to another part of town, and this town was enormous. There had to be a job somewhere. If I could find one around this YMCA, that would work for now. There was a cafeteria in this building and I decided to go there and just look at the prices. Maybe get a cup of coffee and some toast. Suddenly, there was a tremendous noise outside the window, and when I looked out, I realized why my absent roommate chose the other bed. The windows rattled as a large elevated train zoomed past. Sleeping, I thought was going to be tricky.

I readied myself, noted where the floor's shared bathroom was located, and went down the elevator, something else I would need to get used to. I checked out the cafeteria, but skipped the coffee, and went for a walk to familiarize myself with my new neighborhood and look for work.

***

The job I found was as a dishwasher at a close-by restaurant. It didn't pay much, not quite twenty dollars a week, but it was easy work and came with a daily meal, so I could save money on food. I also had Sunday and Monday off, and when I needed to, could pick up some extra money on those days if one of the other dishwashers didn't show up. I started work at two o'clock in the afternoon and used my morning hours to learn about the city. I visited the different neighborhoods and adjusted to taking public transportation. Bus fare was ten cents, and a transfer was free. I traveled many places, viewed the sights, and looked, always searching for another job and a place to live. It was on one of these neighborhood trips I saw a *Looking to Hire* sign in the window of a furniture repair shop.

I had visited this neighborhood before, mainly because the bus I took down a street named *Archer Avenue* stopped at the corner of the cross street, *Western Boulevard*, and on the opposite side was a large park. I enjoyed walking through it, looking at the lagoon (I had to learn what this was), and watching the ducks. It reminded me of the woods behind the farm at Levett, and I appreciated the trees. There were some things I missed. It was a Monday, and I left the park and walked down the side of Western which contained small businesses: a dentist, a law office, a hardware store, and a shoe repair shop. I had time and was glancing into the windows when I saw the *Looking to Hire* sign.

Figuring it wouldn't hurt to ask, I entered and rang the small bell on the counter. An older man came out from behind the door and looked at me over his glasses.

"Can I help you?"

"Yes, Sir, I saw you are hiring, and I would like to know about the job."

He looked at me and chewed the side of his lip. "I need someone who knows about furniture. Maybe a carpenter who has a background in the business."

"Then, I'm your man," I said with much more bravado than I felt. "I've done carpentry work, made furniture, repaired it, and I know what to do."

"Hmm. How old are you, son?"

"Twenty-four, Sir, and I was apprenticed to my father for years. I also worked for a couple years in a small town called Newtown, mostly making furniture, but doing some repairs too."

The man continued to chew his lip. Then he said, "Come on back here. Look at this and tell me what you think."

I walked around the counter, and we entered the shop. There were some tables and chairs piled up in the corner, and his work table was filled. He had been working on a chair, and I could see that there was a broken mortise and tenon joint. The man was checking to see if I knew what to do. I picked up the pieces and examined them.

"Well, the chair is old, but well made. The tenon joint has snapped off and needs replacing, not just repairing because someone attempted to do that already. I'd use a floating tenon for this. But the grain should run the same way as in the original," and I stopped to look at the man.

"Well, son, you talk like you know, but I need to see you at work. Are you willing to give up some of your time to show me what you can do?"

"Yes, Sir, I am. I currently have a job, but I don't start until the afternoons," and I decided to make him the same offer I once made to Mr. Turner. "I'll work the rest of the week in the mornings for you. You won't need to pay me, and if you are satisfied, then hire me. I can be here when you open tomorrow morning," and I waited.

"The shop opens at nine, but I start work at eight in the morning. I'm Joseph Kupper," and he held out his hand.

I shook it and said, "Thomas Allerton, and I'll be here at eight o'clock tomorrow morning, Mr. Kupper."

I worked for him on Tuesday and Wednesday mornings, and on Thursday Mr. Kupper offered me the job in his repair shop. I would make more money than at the restaurant, but would need to provide my own meals and spend money on bus fare. I'd leave from the Wabash Y at seven in the morning, get off the bus at Western, and walk the few streets to the shop, but I was pleased with my good fortune, and glad to be working in a woodshop once more.

***

The commute from the Wabash Y to my job was time-consuming, especially as the weather changed and it grew rainy and cold. Waiting at the bus stop with dozens of others, especially when the bus was filled, the driver couldn't take more passengers, and the wait for another bus was lengthy, was aggravating. I needed to look for a place to live, a room somewhere around the shop. Mr. Kupper saw me reading through the neighborhood papers one day and remarked, "Looking for another job already, Thomas?"

"No, Mr. Kupper. I need a place to live. I've been at the Y for months now, and the commute is getting to me. I know I've been late a few times, and I'm sorry about that, but the buses are crowded and slow. Just looking for a place around here."

He chewed his lip again. "My wife has a friend, a Polish lady who runs a boarding house just a couple streets down on Western. I'll ask her if she knows of a place for you. Let me find out tonight. Now, look at this order for a bookcase. Ever make one?"

I grinned. "Yes, I have," and I began to work.

***

Mrs. Mary Stokowska was my landlady, and while she was not overly friendly or pleasant, she was fair and a decent cook. I decided to pay for board with my room. That included a breakfast of as much coffee as I wanted with toast and oatmeal, and a dinner five nights a week. Lunches and weekend meals were on my own, but the price was right, and I had my own bedroom, one of three, and a shared bath, all on the second floor of her large red-bricked building. There was a separate door and staircase to the second floor, and each week I received clean linens and towels. I was only a few streets away from work which meant I could sleep later in the morning. Life became settled, and while I spent too many nights missing Eddie and cursing Belle, circumstances were, if not good, acceptable. After a Saturday morning working with Mr. Kupper, my favorite afternoon activity was to visit the used bookstore I had discovered and periodically purchase another book to add to my growing collection. I would spend Saturday nights and Sundays reading.

Autumn passed and winter came. Mr. Kupper and his wife invited me to their home for Christmas, but I knew their large family would be coming, and I felt I would be interfering, so I thanked them and turned down the invitation. I invented an old friend who had insisted I visit for the weekend, and because Christmas day was a Sunday, I got away with it. With the lie. I felt bad about making up the story because Mr. Kupper was a fine man and had already given me a raise, but I didn't see any other way out of it. I spent the weekend in my room reading the new book I bought for myself as a Christmas gift. I caught up on some sleep, and listened as Mrs.Stokowska's visiting family laughed and talked in Polish downstairs. I'd gone grocery shopping Saturday morning and ate the sandwiches and some cake I bought. It was a much quieter Christmas than the last few years had been, and I admit, I cried when I thought of Eddie. And, if I was honest, I even missed Belle. I wondered what she was doing, but I didn't have much hope for her future.

The new year came and I felt hopeful again. I had been saving money and needed some new clothes, so I took a trip to the shopping area on Archer Avenue. A large store called the *Archer Avenue Department Store* had opened just a few years back, according to Mr. Kupper, and I could get everything I needed there. I felt like a millionaire buying new clothes, a new winter coat and a pair of shoes. The second-hand items from Mandy's were clothes I had been wearing for years, and they were old and becoming tattered. I tried my new things on again and hung them up in the wardrobe in my room. Then, I wondered where I thought I would wear them. I couldn't wear them to work because I would ruin them. I hadn't made many friends, although I sometimes spoke to Jim who rented the room across from me, and I didn't go places. I decided that I could wear new clothes to work, and then change into my work clothes. At least that way they would get some use, and wearing them would make me feel good. The following Monday I went to work wearing some of my newly bought attire.

I walked in, and Mr. Kupper stopped searching through the papers on the counter and looked at me. Then he raised his eyebrows.

"Well, Mr. Allerton, you look like a fancy business man. Planning to work today or just to look good?"

I grinned at his teasing and held up the knapsack which contained my work clothes. "Thought I'd get some wear out of the new duds, Mr. K. I'll be changing for work. In fact, I'll do that now."

But he stopped me. "Wait for a while, Thomas. Go put an apron on and don't get too dirty. I have something for you to do, and a place to go, and you do look good. We want to present our business as a successful one, and you will do that," and he explained what I would need to do.

A large and prominent law office needed some furniture repairs done. The woman who called said that there were at least half a dozen chairs that needed repairs. They were older chairs, but expensive and useful still, if repaired. Someone needed to visit the office building and examine them and give an estimate for the repairs. They were also considering building additional bookcases, and wanted the work done there. Mr. Kupper was sending me to do the examination and estimate, and I needed to be there at ten-thirty.

"I would go myself, but looking the way you do, you should go. Besides, I trust you, and if they hire us to do the work, you'll be completing it. Once you check things out, ask to use their telephone and call me before you give them anything in writing. Meantime, that inventory you started needs to get finished. You should be able to walk to the building which is down on Archer Avenue, and you can leave at ten. I need to finish the upholstery on Mrs. Adams' Queen Anne chair."

We worked at our separate tasks, and at ten o'clock, I left. It was a mild late February day, and I enjoyed the walk. When I got to the large building, I took the elevator (Thank you Wabash Y for teaching me how to work it.) to the third floor and looked for the door. I knocked, and then walked it to a large outer office. A woman sitting at the front desk greeted me.

"Good morning, I'm from Kupper's Furniture Repair Shop, here to give an estimate on some repairs," I said, trying to sound business-like.

"Oh yes. Miss Becker said you would be in. Please have a seat, and I'll call for her," and she picked up the telephone, dialed a number and spoke into it. "Miss Becker, the furniture repair man is here. Yes, I will," and she hung up.

"Please have a seat. Miss Becker is on her way," and she smiled and ignored me.

I didn't sit, but stood waiting for this woman. It took about ten minutes until the door to another office opened, and she came out.

That was the day I met Carolina Becker.

Chapter 16   1898

While there wasn't as much call for casket building due to the new undertaker having set up his furniture shop and funeral services close by, in the next town, the young man and his grandfather still found neighbors who preferred the workmanship and lower prices of their efforts. Then there was the tradition of having both parents or grandparents or a child buried in the same type of casket as other family members when they were placed in the ground at the town cemetery or the family burial plot. The Allertons continued to offer the service that had been started almost a dozen years before when the town's original undertaker had decided to move further north. The grandson had become almost as expert as his grandfather. They worked together on this new casket, actually, a *coffin*, for there is a difference.

"It's the shape, you see," explained the grandfather, "the casket is a box shape with four sides and a top and bottom. The coffin has six sides and the top and bottom. Most folks aim for something simpler, so these *eternity boxes* are what we make."

"The coffin is shaped like a body," commented the grandson.

"It is, boy, it is."

Not much was said as they completed the sanding, trimming, and finishing of this project. They knew the process, having made one exactly like it four years previously when the grandmother, Mary Allerton took sick, and the town doctor told her family to "make her comfortable and prepare for her passing". Her husband and grandson did that. They took on her chores, spent as much time as possible with her, and attempted cheerfulness. Within a month of taking to bed, the grandmother pushed the clouds of Heaven away and entered her eternal home. During the waiting time, her husband and grandson had worked on her coffin, using white oak, not the usual pine. The oak would not stop the natural decay, but would delay it, and the workability of the wood was unproblematic. Special trim, carved by her husband, was placed on the edges, creating a fanciful look, one that Mary Allerton might not have approved of, being an unpretentious woman, if she had ever seen it.

The coffin currently being made was for the grandfather. The same town doctor listened to his heart, asked about his weight loss, monitored his fainting spells and weaknesses, and when pressed into truthfulness, acknowledged that the grandfather would soon join his wife in pushing away the Heavenly clouds. The grandfather sat still and listened. He was stoic and accepting of the pronouncement and only concerned about breaking the news to his grandson who had just turned seventeen.

One evening, after sharing a simple meal of bacon, goat cheese, and bread, all washed down with the morning's left-over coffee, a serious discussion was held. The grandfather and his grandson spoke together about his will, his wishes, and his worries. The will conferred it all to the grandson; the wishes were to be buried by the grandson next to the grandmother; the worries centered around the young boy having to become nursemaid to an ailing old man. However, the grandfather hung on until the boy's eighteenth year, a kind neighbor helped with the burial preparations, and the grandfather, ever considerate, simply dropped dead one morning as he went to feed the chickens.

The small farm had become smaller after the grandmother's death. She had kept some goats for milking and knew how to handle them, how to keep them steady for the task. Once she was gone, the goats were given to a neighbor with the understanding that every few days, a couple quarts of milk would be sent to the grandfather. That worked out. Then there were the two horses. One was sold since the feeding, watering, and grooming two of them took time away from the necessary carpentry work. The grandfather was sad to see the horse go, but needed only one for the wagon. The chickens stayed, and the two males took turns cleaning, watering, feeding, and collecting the eggs, some of which they traded to the farmer who had the goats in exchange for some periodic cheese. But the grandmother had tended the animals, and her care of them was missed.

Gardening was also an issue. A truck patch was behind the small house, and when the grandmother was alive, she managed that too. Vegetables were plentiful in the summer and fall. Tomatoes, beans, corn, new potatoes, and spring onions filled the table. Extras were canned for use throughout the winter. She grew herbs and dried them. She made sure that the bulb onions, spinach, and kale used in winter were planted at the right time. "Do it right." she used to say, "and you'll have them all year." And she did it right. The apple and pear tree produced fruit used for fresh eating, baking, and canning. Blackberries grew on hardy bushes towards the end of the garden, and once she was gone, so was her blackberry jam. Both much missed. The grandmother always bragged she was a better farmer than her husband. He agreed, but then, he used to tease she couldn't make a blanket chest or whittle a cane. The small farm was a smooth-running operation when the grandmother was alive.

When she died, the grandson was just fourteen and in seventh grade. She wanted him to complete eighth-grade and get the certificate which stated so. The boy's dead father had never completed his schooling, and she felt a need to push his son. The boy wanted to quit after grade six to become a full-time apprentice in his grandfather's woodshop, but he was talked into continuing school, mostly to please his Granny. However, once she was gone, it didn't take much to talk his grandfather into letting him leave school.

"Son, you only have one more year. Your grandmother wanted you to get that piece of paper, and I hate to disappoint her."

"I know, Pa, but Granny is gone, and it's just the two of us. How can you do your work in the shop and take care of the house and the animals and the garden by yourself? If I'm here all day and not at school, I can help, and we can still work in the shop. You said I'm getting better, and anyway, you were fourteen when you started as an apprentice."

The boy made sense. The grandfather had no idea how everything was going to get done without his wife. The boy was almost an adult. He was taller than his grandfather, and he was still growing. He was strong, and it had been a struggle to get him to continue seventh-grade when the school term started, and the boy and the new teacher did not seem to get along. It was true that Granny would never know. They would need to eliminate some of the animals, and both needed to care for the garden. They might make it, but only if they worked together. A decision was made. Seventh grade ended.

The two of them struggled with the cooking. Breakfast was easy: a drink of water and a quick bite of whatever was left over from the previous night held them until the morning chores were done. Then eggs and coffee, and the work began. Late afternoon they managed some supper, augmented with apples and pears taken, in season, from the trees. Before dark, the night chores needed completing along with washing up, and remembering to feed the inside cat (good mouser), and Molly the dog. All the dogs were named Molly. It was easier when a new one came along. The cat had no name. Not that she would have come when called anyway.

The Hampton family down the way took pity on the two males and sent cooking help. They had "an over-abundance of females", as Mr. Hampton called it when referring to his four daughters, and the youngest, Clara, was the grandson's friend from school. Once it was discovered by Mrs. Hampton, that the two males were struggling to eat properly because they lacked the basic skills, Clara and her older sister, Jennifer, the one who was just married, were sent down to spend some time with the grandfather and the boy, and give them basic cooking lessons. There was nothing fancy: stews and soups mostly, but there was that important lesson in baking bread and making cornbread. It was discovered that bread-baking required a proficiency that neither the grandfather nor the grandson had. Their bread never turned out like the grandmother's excellent loaves, but it was deemed eatable. Cornbread was easier, and it appeared often at supper and the next morning's early breakfast. Pies, cakes, and the molasses cookies that were a favorite, became fond memories. The boy did make a few attempts at the cookies, but he burned the cookie tin and his hand, and the cookies never tasted anything like the grandmother's cookies, so he stopped wasting time and ingredients. Sweets were eaten only if offered by neighbors.

The years after the grandmother's passing eventually evened themselves out. The chores, cooking, and cleaning were shared, and it mostly got done. The house was never as clean as before. Their clothes weren't either. And the food simply sustained them. But they worked as long as possible in the woodshop, and the boy grew and learned, and by the time he was seventeen, was almost as competent as his grandfather. They made a living together and created the blanket chests which were sold in the general store to both townspeople and the few out-of-towners who stopped by. Every year, fence posts were ordered, houses demanded moldings and baseboards, and the occasional chest of drawers or bed-frame was needed. Winter carving and whittling netted wooden toys, birdhouses, canes, and keepsake boxes which were also sold at the general store. And of course, the caskets, those eternity boxes, brought in needed cash. There were extras of all sizes stacked around the side wall of the shop. All ready for the first, and last, use.

And the boy, now the young man, would have to do everything alone when his grandfather was gone. The entire farm: the garden, the animals, the woodshop, the cooking, the laundry, the care of the house and himself, would be his to complete. He was just eighteen when the old man fell in front of the chicken coop, spilling the chicken feed and laying there for the better part of an hour until the howling of Molly finally caused the grandson to stop the weeding in the back garden and come to see what the commotion was about.

The grandfather's funeral was simple. The neighbor who had been given the goats came and helped the grandson place his grandfather into the casket they had worked on together. Being late summer, the ground was soft enough to dig the grave next to Granny's spot, and a simple prayer was said. The Hamptons with their daughters, Jennifer, and Clara, were in attendance, and some of the area farmers took an hour from their work to pay respects. The men pitched in to lower the box into the hole, after which the spot was filled in with the soft earth. A couple of stones marked the place and gave the grandson some times to have a proper marker made. The Hampton women had brought some casseroles and bread and some fruit pies for a luncheon which was held in the small kitchen area of the farmhouse. Upon leaving, the men shook the young man's hand and wished him luck. Clara kissed his cheek.

The young man had a plan. He and Clara had grown up together, gone to school sitting across from each other, traveled jointly to Sunday School, and he was sure they would spend the rest of their days as a couple. But he was only eighteen, and Clara was barely sixteen, and Mr. Hampton didn't think she should marry at such a delicate age, being his youngest and all. However, he was not against finding a place and a husband for this fourth daughter in a year or so, if the two were still willing then.

They would be. They discussed it. Clara spent a few hours each week at the small farm, cooking for her fiancé, and straightening out and cleaning the small house which would soon be hers. This allowed the young man to work in his shop, filling the orders for the fence posts and door frames, and earning money for necessities. As he finished the projects, he made additional caskets to place along the woodshop sides and took his turn weeding the garden and caring for the animals.

He worked hard and steady and by himself. For over a year, he worked alone except for a few hours a week with Clara, and that time left its mark on him. He had no one to speak with and acquired a habit of silence and introspection. He did think. He thought about the past, trying to remember his mother, and remembering all too well, his father. He missed the grandmother sometimes, but really missed the grandfather, and on some days, he walked to the family gravesite to look over the stones he had placed on the graves and move the crabapples that had fallen from the grass.

Life seemed unfair. He was struggling. The adjustment was difficult, and he waited out the time until he and Clara could be married. Someone with whom he could speak and interact. Another person to take over some of these chores. A presence who would be a help and a support. He thought that if he had any belief in what others called the *Almighty*, he would call Clara's eventual presence a *Godsend*. But he didn't. He just wanted the time to pass. "Don't hurry the future," is what his grandfather used to say, but the young man did want to hurry it. Waiting in the present while thinking of the past and hoping for the future was trying.

Chapter 17   1928

Carolina Becker was two years older than me, and she had been born in Poland. She and her family: her father Walter, mother Ola, and brother Jan, had come to this country when she was two, in 1903, the year I was born, but she no longer had a family. Her brother had been killed in France during the Great War when he was just eighteen. She told me that his death so affected her mother that, in 1919, when she became ill from the Spanish flu, she told Carolina she didn't care to live and just wanted to go and be with her son in Heaven. When her mother died, Carolina and her father lived together until heart failure took his life in 1926, two years before I met her. Carolina had some cousins and an aunt and uncle who lived on Chicago's north side, but she didn't see them often. She roomed with another girl, Sandy, in a small apartment within walking distance of her office, and she answered to the nickname, *Lina*.

Of course, I didn't learn this all at once, but gradually, as Lina and I got to know each other. I was hesitant about seeing her as anything but a friend. We formed a friendly relationship that centered around books and travel. We wandered throughout Chicago, learning about the city and its history and had a good time doing it. Lina was different than the other women I had known. She was not frail and angelic and blonde like Ava; nor was she elegantly mysterious like Mrs. Vogel; and there was not the wildness and carefreeness to her that had been present in Belle. Lina was sensible, and smart, and seemly, and I felt at ease with her. She had graduated from a Chicago high school with bookkeeping and clerical skills, and then took some business school classes that were open to women at one of the city colleges. She started working for the Baum Legal Firm when she was just twenty, and over the last eight years, worked her way up from stenographer/ typist to the office manager. I admired her from the start.

Mr. Kupper sent me to work at the chair (and one desk) repairs on Thursday and Friday. "Ask them about Saturday work," he said, "and if they need you, then go there instead of coming to the shop."

When I mentioned Saturday, Lina went to ask her boss about the work since they normally didn't work on Saturdays. She came back to the room where I was finishing up one of the chairs.

"Mr. Baum said that you working here on Saturday is acceptable. He thought that if you were here without any other employees, you could get started on the bookcases he wants in the conference room. I'll be here to open the door, and stay until you are done for the day. Will that work, Mr. Allerton?"

I said it would and told her I felt bad taking Saturday away from her and creating another work day. But Lina said she had some paperwork to complete and would bring a book with her. Besides, she didn't mind because she would be getting paid for the day.

I showed up at eight o'clock that Saturday morning, just as she did, and we entered the building. She held a book in her hand, and I asked what she was reading. She showed me the title, *The Great Gatsby*, and we talked while in the elevator about the book and its author, neither of which I knew. She opened the office, pointing out where she would be if I needed something, and I went into the room where the furniture was stored and began the repairs. About noon, I began taking measurements and creating plans for the bookcases, and she came in to talk to me.

"Mr. Allerton, I'm going to call the deli across the street and get some lunch. Mr. Baum said to ask what you would like and to order it, so what would you like for lunch?"

When the sandwiches and coffee came, the two of us ate together in the conference room and spoke of reading and books. I told her about the used bookstore I frequented, and she was glad to learn of it. That was the first conversation we had, and I was surprised at how comfortable I felt. We left about three o'clock because I could do no more work until the additional material and tools were delivered. I offered to walk her to her apartment which was just a few streets from the office building. We talked all the way, and I decided Lina was someone with whom I would like to have more conversations.

I probably took longer than necessary to create the bookcases. Each additional day I was there, I could see her and spend time with her. Finally, I knew I should not linger longer at the job; Mr. Kupper was wondering why it was taking so long, and he needed me back at the shop. I finished up, and as Lina brought me the final papers to sign and the check for Mr. Kupper, I asked if sometime she would like to go to a movie with me. I was nervous about this. She was educated and knowledgeable, and I wasn't. But we had enjoyed talking, and there had been a few more Saturdays when she and I were the only ones in the building, and I looked forward to those lunchtime discussions. She hesitated for just a bit, and then said, "Yes, Thomas, I think that sounds like fun," and I was elated. I had a reason now to wear my new clothes.

That was the start of our friendship. I began to look for movies and plays and places to visit with Lina, and when I saw that a place called the Goodman Theatre was producing a Shakespeare play I had read: *A Midsummer Night's Dream*, I asked Mr. Kupper how to go about getting tickets for it.

"Let me ask my wife," he said, "Sometimes her women's church group goes to those things. Personally, I'd rather sit at home and listen to my radio. *The Dodge Victory Hour* is very entertaining, and a new show called *Amos `n` Andy* makes me laugh. Will let you know tomorrow."

He did, and I got two tickets, and we went. I tried to act like I was familiar with all the details and finer points of theater going, but I had never been to one before. Neither had Lina, and we laughed as we learned what to do together. That was in the spring.

We went to some fancy picture palaces, especially the Downtown Chicago Theater where ushers led us to our seats, and we saw movies like *A Race for Life*, *Fools for Luck*, and *Legion of the Condemned*. The *Race* movie made me sad because Rin-Tin-Tin was in it, and I remembered my dog, Molly. The *Legion* movie made Lina cry because it was about World War I, and she thought about her brother dying in France. But we both laughed at W.C. Fields in the *Fools* movie, and decided that we would try to see other movies starring him. I worked most Saturday mornings at the shop, and we generally went to a Saturday afternoon movie because it was thirty-five cents and not the fifty cents charged at night. I felt strange about *going Dutch*, which is what Lina said we should do since we were just friends. Sometimes I insisted on paying for both of us, especially when we did things I wanted to try. Once I wanted to have some Chinese food, so we went to the Joy Lo King Restaurant on West Randolph. We had some delicious hot tea with our dinner of chop suey, something I had never tasted, and relished the sweet cookie-like wafers which were served afterwards. We took advantage of the museums in Chicago, and Lina knew which ones offered free admittance. My favorite was the Field Museum of Natural History, but hers was the Art Institute, and we visited both often.

We were excited to see some of the new talkies that came out. In late September, we saw Al Jolson in *The Singing Fool*, and while the sounds and music we heard with the movie was amazing, I could barely sit through it. Afterward, even though it was early on a Saturday and normally we would stop at one of our favorite diners for some flapjacks, I told Lina I didn't feel good, and I took her home and walked back to my room.

I walked slowly and thought about my life. I couldn't tell Lina what the real problem was. I hadn't told her much about me at all. She knew I came from a small town in central Illinois, had been trained as a carpenter and furniture maker by my father, and had tramped around for years. She didn't know I had been married to Ava or I had two sons who died. She didn't know anything about Belle, and she certainly didn't know about Mrs. Vogel and my time with her. I hadn't spoken to anyone, including Lina. about the facts of my life. And Lina had not pressured me about it. She had to have been curious, but she never questioned me, and when I grew silent about a subject, she changed it. She was understanding and gentle. She tolerated my silences and allowed me my periodic sullenness. I began to appreciate her more and to value her companionship. To be truthful, I was feeling more than just a friendship towards her, and it frightened me.

The Jolson movie made me think about Eddie. In the movie, the main character had a faithless wife who took away the son they had. The poor little boy, named *Sonny*, ended up in the hospital, dying. I could barely sit through the movie. It wasn't exactly like my life, but it was close enough, and the little three-year-old boy in the movie had dark hair like Eddie's, and my heart was breaking as I sat there. I know Lina was wiping her eyes, and I quickly wiped my tears, and I knew I needed to be by myself. As I walked back to my room, I made a decision. I would go back to Stone City and visit Eddie's grave.

The following week, I asked Mr. Kupper if I could have Saturday morning off because I wanted to visit the same pretend friend who had invited me for Christmas. He agreed, and on Friday, I used his telephone to call Lina and tell her I needed to be gone for the weekend, and we couldn't go out as we had planned. She never questioned where I was going or acted upset, but simply said, "OK, Tom. I'll see you another time. Bye for now," and I was grateful.

***

Early Saturday morning, I traveled to the LaSalle Street Station and bought a round-trip ticket to Stone City. I wasn't sure where Eddie was buried but would find out. When I got off the train, I made my way to the funeral parlor to talk to Mr. Overton, or anyone who could tell me where he was. When I arrived, the building was open and activity was evident. People were moving things into place, and setting flowers around and there was obvious preparation for a wake to be held later, and in retrospect, I was lucky. As I walked in, it occurred to me that the funeral parlor could have been closed, and I wouldn't be able to see Eddie. Mr. Overton was seated in his office and looked up when I knocked on the door.

"Yes, may I be of assistance?"

"Mr. Overton, I'm Thomas Allerton. My son Eddie, Louis Edward Allerton, was buried last year in late summer. I need to know which cemetery he's in."

Mr. Overton, to his credit, didn't ask questions or say anything about the fact that I had stalked out of his business during Eddie's wake, or about the heated conversation Belle and I had just outside his office which could easily be heard by him, or that I had come in and counted out the money to pay for the funeral and was hardly civil to him. He just nodded and stood up and went to a large cabinet in the corner of his office and opened a drawer. He searched through the files and found a paper which he quickly read. He turned to me and said, "Your son is buried at the Woody Oak Cemetery out on Cass Street. He is in section 4, lot 416. Do you need me to write that down for you?"

"Section 4, lot 416. No, I'll remember. Thank you," and I held out my hand to him.

He shook it and said, "Losing a child, especially one so young, is heartbreaking. I am sorry, Mr. Allerton, for your loss."

I couldn't speak, so I just nodded and turned to leave the building. I stood outside and took a while to compose myself, and then realized I had no way of getting to the cemetery. But I had money now and could hire someone to take me. A taxi car was needed, and I would have to go back into the building to ask Mr. Overton to call one for me. I sighed and turned back in to ask the favor. Mr. Overton simply picked up his telephone, called the taxi car company and told me one would be there in twenty minutes, and I was welcomed to wait in his office. I thanked him again and waited outside.

When the car came, I got in and told the driver where I wanted to go. "I'll need you to wait for me. I know you'll keep the meter running, and that is fine. Will you wait?"

"Sure, Buddy, I'll wait. Who you goin' to see?"

"My son," and the driver looked in the mirror at me, and neither of us spoke the remainder of the trip.

We got to the cemetery, and it was large and confusing. I didn't know where to look for Eddie. We couldn't find section 4, and we drove around for a long time. Finally, the driver said, "Look. There's a man working on the lawn. Think he's a caretaker. Let me drive there and ask him," and he did.

The man was able to point the way to us, and guided me to the correct lot area. I thanked him, and we drove over two lanes. It turned out we weren't far from the section and the area. The driver pulled over and said, "Go on, take your time. I'll wait here."

I walked over to the graves which were behind a small metal sign labeled: *Lots 400-450*, and began to walk and count. There, next to:

Loretta 'Lottie' Haversome
1865-1927
Loving Mother and Grandmother

was a small stone with the inscription:

Louis Edward Allerton
1924-1927
Repose en Paix

I stood there and couldn't breathe. I didn't move for at least ten minutes, and then I knelt and ran my hands over the stone, over the words. I read them repeatedly, and I didn't bother wiping the tears from my face. There were a few weeds around the stone, and I pulled them out, remembering doing the same thing for my mother's and my brothers' graves before I left Levett. That seemed so long ago. I leaned forward and kissed the stone and rested my head on it. I leaned down to Loretta 'Lottie' Haversome's grave and whispered to her, "Please watch over my son. He needs a loving grandmother," and finally, I stood up.

The taxi driver had been watching me. I wiped my face, walked back to the taxi, and got in. He turned to look at me and quietly asked, "Back to the funeral parlor?"

"No," I answered, "Please take me to the train station. Can we get there by five o'clock? That's when my train leaves."

"Sure, Buddy, I'll get you there," and he did.

We stopped in front of the station at a quarter to five, and I reached into my pants pocket as I asked, "How much for today?"

The driver shook his head as he spoke. "Nothing, Buddy. I didn't have much to do today anyway. Sorry about your son."

I was astounded, and grateful, but I took out a ten-dollar bill and as I got out of the back, I put it on the passenger seat in the front. I looked at him and attempted a smile. "Thank you," is what I croaked out, and I walked quickly into the station to catch the last train into Chicago that night.

***

I stayed in bed all Sunday thinking. The next week, I was so silent at work, Mr. Kupper asked if something was wrong or if I was sick. "If you don't feel well, tell me what's wrong, and I'll tell my wife. She can fix you up with some remedy. She's good at that."

I assured him that I was well. Just had some things on my mind. I didn't call Lina that weekend. I didn't want her to think I was angry, but I didn't want to talk to her just yet. I let the next week go by, and the following Friday, I called her from Mr. Kupper's telephone and asked if she wanted to go to lunch Saturday afternoon after I finished working.

"I'm glad to hear from you. Yes, Tom, that would be fine. I hope everything is OK. I was worried about you. Do you want to see a movie or visit the Field Museum?"

"Not tomorrow," I said, "Just lunch and maybe we can talk. I'll pick you up at your apartment about twelve-thirty," and the plans were made.

After work the following day, I walked over to Lina's apartment and rang her doorbell. She peeked out and called to me that she'd be right down, and when she walked down the stairs, my heart jumped. I realized how glad I was to see her. She had become important to me, and I was going to be honest with her. I had spent the last two weeks thinking about what I was going to tell her; what I would admit to her. I decided to begin with the most private, sensitive part.

We walked to one of the diners at which we regularly ate, and I asked for the booth at the back. The waitress led us there, and we sat down. We took time to examine the lunch menu, and when the waitress and the coffee appeared, we ordered. The coffee cups steamed in front of us, and I looked across the booth at Lina. She smiled and waited for me to speak.

"I need to tell you some things," I said, "and I want to start with Mrs. Vogel."

Chapter 18   1893

The boy crouched forward in the wagon, moving his shoulders around, stretching his back. It had been a long, fifty-mile journey from their house to the sawmill in Lytleville where he and his grandfather had traveled to get the load of ordered white oak. This was the fourth day of the trip, and while they were close to home, he wondered if he could stand any more traveling. The trip there had been quick, but coming home with the wagonload of wood was taking longer. He was hot and dirty and anxious for Granny's good cooking. He had been warned, when he begged to go, that this was no pleasure trip, and was given the option of staying home, but he was thirteen and anxious for adventure.

"Pa, we're home soon, right?"

His grandfather glanced sideways at him and grinned. Over the past years, his grandson had taken to calling him *Pa*, and while the implied relationship wasn't legal, it was authentic and spoke of authority. And the boy reminded him of his son.

"Soon, boy. Less than two hours now. Trip back is always slower and harder because of the load pulled. Horse is tired too. Once we're home, we'll rest and eat. Then we need to move this lumber into the back of the building. Trip's not over until it's stacked the right way. Grab that jar of water under the seat, will you? And how about leading the wagon for a turn?"

The boy grabbed the jar, and the wagon was halted while they both drank from it. They got down to stand and stretch their back and legs, and when they climbed back onto the wagon, the reins were handed over. *Pa* took off his hat, encouraging a breeze to blow through his long, sweaty graying hair which was thinning on the top. He pushed the hair back, returned the hat to its rightful place, and the boy clicked his tongue and said, "Git, now," in the same manner as his grandfather.

"Going to get some of this mess cut off soon. I'll ask your grandma to cut it. How about that mop of yours? Ready for a cut?"

The boy shrugged his shoulders not caring. It was late summer, and concern about his personal appearance wasn't on his mind. He was concentrating on the reins in his hand, wishing he had some of those gloves he had seen at the general store they had visited. That would save his hands from the red lines he knew would appear, but he didn't grumble. He held tighter to the reins and sat up straighter, determined to show he was grown. He had something he needed to talk about with Pa, and was just waiting for the right time. So, he continued to look ahead at the road, sit straight, hold the reins, and not complain.

The boy sifted through his thoughts. During the years he had lived with his grandparents, he had come to learn and appreciate certain skills. His grandfather was a carpenter, a proficient with wood, and the boy took to this effort. He was fascinated with the tools: the planes, the rasps, the files and scrapers, the saws and hammers and wrenches. Astounding items were created with them, and as Pa worked, he watched and learned. He also, although not consciously, wanted to cultivate a relationship with this man who taught him and cared for him. His parents were gone; the mother dying when he was a baby, and the father dying when he was young. Even when alive, they formed no bond due to the father's deep interest and connection with spirits. The liquid kind. So, movement from the appellation *Grandfather* to *Pa* was imperceptibly done.

Woods surrounded the area, and the boy had come to identify and appreciate various trees and their uses. He and Pa would walk the wooded areas searching for useful fallen branches of the staghorn sumac. After a storm was the choicest time to collect them and place them in the sun behind the workshop to dry a while. The wood was good to work with, to create small items such as boxes for keepsakes or carved wooden animal toys. Sumac needed careful sanding, and during cold winters when ice and snow prevented outside work, proficiency was attained. Red cedar was used for the blanket chests Pa made and sold, and the boy had used some of the larger leftover pieces for carving, with his most serious project being the birdhouse that hung from the apple tree in the yard. The white oak was most useful for cabinets and floor planks and fence posts, all which Pa made. Of course, white pine was a favorite due to the ease of workability. Crates and boxes came from this wood, and occasionally Pa was asked to complete baseboards and moldings for new houses. And the caskets, of course, which, when made, lined the side of the workshop, ready for use and purchase. Both large and small caskets were built. Smaller ones being in more demand during the summer months when fevers assailed the young.

At thirteen, the boy had definite ideas about his future. His plan was to work at the small farm his grandparents owned and which would become his and continue the creation of wood commodities. He was familiar enough with various woods and his carving was improving, but he knew that additional knowledge and experience was needed. He was expected to travel to the schoolhouse daily during the months of the year it was in service. He left the farm at eight-fifteen in the morning, after his morning chores were completed, and did not get back to the farm until after three in the afternoon. Prime time for Pa's work in the woodshop. Time he could be, should be, with Pa, learning and practicing his skills. His grandfather had worked as an apprentice, a journeyman, then married, and had a family he left to fight in the divided country's war. Living in the small town of Levett, and being experienced and expert in the wood crafts allowed him to set up his own business. And it was successful enough to support his family. The boy wanted to do the same. So, he would need to quit school.

He had just completed sixth grade. He was sure there was not much more to learn. His time would be better spent learning from Pa and practicing wood-related competences and proficiencies. And schooling took away from time required. After all, he knew the basics of reading and writing, and, frankly, saw little need for them. Additional reading and the rules of grammar were a waste of time. Verb cases and principal parts and punctuation were pointless. He knew the geography of Champaign County because he had traveled it with Pa, and now he knew how to get to the Lytleville sawmill and lumber yard when additional cut wood planks were needed. He knew a bit about the history of the United States and of Illinois, and since he had no plans to move away from his current home, additional geography lessons were unneeded. Arithmetic was useful, but it was practiced continually in his measuring and determining cuts and installations and planning. The boy could figure out costs, expenses, charges, and losses because he had been helping to do it for years, and Pa relied on him. Besides, this year, a new teacher, a man, would take the place of Miss Daisy Winslow. It was rumored that he was not as easygoing and lenient as Miss Winslow had been. That was not good news. If only Pa would understand. The school year was a few weeks away, and he needed to have this important conversation soon. He continued to watch the road and decided to broach the subject.

"Pa?"

"Yes, boy?"

"I've been thinking about my future and what I want to do."

"Good. Always important to have plans."

The boy glanced sideways at his grandfather whose hat was pulled down onto his face and whose arms were folded across his chest. He hoped he had the right words for this matter.

"I want to do what you do: work with wood and make things."

"Well, you are learning. Keep it up."

"But I want to do it all the time."

"That time will come. Don't hurry the future."

The boy took a breath and thought. He wasn't making his case and would need to just come out and say what he wanted to do.

"Pa, I think I've had enough schooling. I learned lots of things, but nothing that will help me do what you do. You said you were about my age when you were an apprentice, so I think I should just help you at the shop, stay at the farm and not go back to school this term," and he took a deep breath and felt the quick beating of his heart.

For two minutes, there was no sound or movement from Pa. Then he sat up and pushed his hat back and looked at the boy who was trying to look older. Pa sighed and then spoke.

"I was almost fifteen when I started my apprenticeship. Things were different in those days. Schooling was not thought so necessary and everyone worked. The world has changed, boy, and whether you think you need more schooling or not, the bottom fact is that your grandmother has a mind to you getting that eighth-grade certificate. She is determined to see you through it, and because her health is not good, I'd like to see her get this wish. Finish school. There's plenty of time for you to work after that. It's just two more years. Plenty of time to work on those eternity boxes."

"But 'almost fifteen' means you were fourteen, and I'm just a year younger. I'll be that age in a few months, Pa. What good is that certificate? My own pa never got one, did he?"

"Nope, he didn't. And that could be why your grandmother is so set on you getting one. Don't want her to have a conniption fit because you decide not to finish it. It's just two years, Gid. You can continue to work with me after school and on weekends and summer. I'll call you my apprentice if you want. Finish up the schooling. Get the certificate. Besides, your little friend, Clara would miss you. Right?" and Pa grinned at the boy who blushed.

"Naw. She's young. Over a year younger than me. Maybe closer to two years. She's just a baby."

"Babies grow up, Gid. That they do. You are young and more schooling can't hurt. Your Granny has been through enough in her life, and it's a small thing to do to make her happy," and Pa pulled his hat down and slouched back into the seat. The conversation was over.

There was no more talk about quitting school the rest of the way home. The boy knew when he should be quiet, and he decided that enough was said for today. No sense in bringing it up again. There would be another day and another time. He continued to guide the horse home to the farm and let the conversation play through his mind. He supposed two years weren't that long and it would make his granny happy. Maybe he'd give it some thought. Maybe.

Chapter 19   1929-1930

I bought tickets for a play called *The Front Page* at the Enlanger Theatre on December 30, 1928, and I told Lina we would go out for a late dinner afterwards at the Italian Village to celebrate the end of the year. That night was cold, but the restaurant was only about three streets away, so we walked fast and got there quick. It was crowded, and our seating was delayed, but the waiting area was warm and cheerful and smelled delicious. She ordered pasta and red sauce, and I wanted to try the eggplant parmesan, and we shared our dinners. For dessert, we sipped coffee, ate cannoli, and talked about our wedding.

It wasn't going to be large or fancy. We couldn't afford it, had no family to invite, and wanted to marry by the end of January. Lina's roommate, Sandy, said she could get someone to take Lina's place, but the new girl needed to move in by then. We couldn't live together in my small boarding room, so we were searching for another apartment or even a small house to rent. It was the middle of winter, and moving was going to be difficult, especially if there was additional snow. So, we were talking about what to do.

"Umm, this is delicious," Lina said as she chewed, "I wonder how expensive cannoli would be to serve instead of a wedding cake?"

I took the last bite and chewed. "I'm not sure Mrs. Kupper would take kindly to that. She has everything planned. Mr. K. comes in daily to tell me about the plans. She is excited about doing this for us, and I think we should just go along with her. Don't you?"

"Sure," Lina finished her coffee. "I am grateful for the Kupper's offer. I was just thinking out loud."

Lina and I had spent Thanksgiving Day and Christmas Day with Mr. and Mrs. Kupper and their family. This year, I didn't lie about a pretend friend, and Mr. Kupper insisted we come. After Thanksgiving dinner, Lina and I announced our engagement and plans to marry in the new year, and that was all Mrs. Kupper needed. She knew neither of us had family, and Lina's aunt and uncle had moved to Milwaukee. She insisted on giving a dinner at the Kupper house after our wedding, and celebrating with a wedding cake and sparkling grape juice toasts. She supported Prohibition. She was only disappointed we weren't going to have a big church ceremony, but planned on a City Hall marriage. Both Lina and I gave in to her determination to host a dinner on Saturday,

February 2 in the new year. Getting married before then wouldn't be an issue, but finding a place to live was.

We spent New Year's Day at Lina's apartment with Sandy and a couple of Lina's friends from work. I asked one of the men at my boarding house, Jim, to come with me, and the six of us had a great time laughing and playing card games. Lina mentioned the difficulty we were having in finding a place to live, and everyone there said they would be on the lookout for an apartment for us. It was a pleasant way to spend the day, and afterwards, Jim and I walked Lina's coworkers to the bus stop, and then we went back to the boarding house.

It was a lucky thing Lina invited her coworkers to the apartment. They spread the news, and the women at Baum Legal all began to watch for available apartments or houses for us. That was how we got one, and how I got a part-time job which, by 1930, I would need. A week into the new year, Lina was called into Mr. Baum's office.

"Miss Becker, please sit down," he asked, "Congratulations on your coming marriage. I know you have been with us for eight years now, and we at this firm esteem your work and appreciate your loyalty."

Lina told me this was a surprise to her, and she thought she was going to be fired. Just the week before Christmas, two of the stenographer/typists were let go. One was constantly late, and the other was just a poor worker. She said she sat down and could barely keep still.

"Thank you, Mr. Baum," was all she could get out.

Then he proceeded to surprise her. And me.

"It occurs to me that I have a chance to solve a couple of problems here. My brother, Gerald, and I own three two-flats right around 38th and Rockwell, not too far from here. We are in need of a manager and handy-man, and since one of the apartments in the first two-flat is empty, I would like to offer it to you and your fiancé, Mr. Allerton, right? Yes, Mr. Allerton. I am aware of Mr. Allerton's handy skills, and if he is willing to work nights and weekends taking care of whatever problems come up in the buildings, I can offer the apartment to you at a very reduced rent. The apartments go for between fifteen and twenty dollars a month, and the one I am offering you has three bedrooms and is quite spacious. If I were to charge you seven dollars a month, and Mr. Allerton is willing to work as needed, would you consider that?"

Lina said she almost jumped up and down, but she maintained her composure and replied, "That does sound fair, Mr. Baum. May I discuss it with Thomas tonight and let you know tomorrow?"

"Of course, Miss Becker. And, I am assuming you will continue to work for us after you are married?"

"Yes, Sir, that is my plan," and Lina was delighted that Mr. Baum understood about working women. It helped that he had three daughters, and the older two held jobs.

We were thrilled with the offer, and when we visited the apartment, we were amazed at its size. There were three bedrooms, a bathroom, a large living room, a spacious kitchen with a back porch whose door opened to a small yard. I was delighted when I saw the built-in bookcases in the living room. Between Lina's book collection and mine, we had a great start for our own library.

We married on Friday, January 25 at City Hall and spent Friday night in Downtown Chicago at the Drake Hotel. The room was elegant and stylish, and if the cost hadn't been so exorbitant (five dollars per night), we might have stayed for two nights. But Saturday afternoon, Lina and I traveled back to our new apartment on Rockwell Street (which had a bed and a kitchen table and chairs, but no other furniture) and began our lives together.

***

The Kuppers would continue to play a role in our lives after the wedding dinner they gave for us. The evening was carefully planned and managed by Mrs. Kupper, and it was great fun. After the dinner, Mr. Kupper took me aside and told me that should I need anything… advice, instruction, direction in marriage issues, I could come to him. I thanked him, and allowed him to believe this was my first marriage. Both Lina and I decided it was best no one knew my past. I reflected on the father-figures in my life: Mr. Turner, Mr. Kupper, John, the foreman at the furniture factory, even the taxi driver who drove me out to Eddie's grave and didn't want to take money for it, and wondered that they all seemed to be empathetic and understanding, more so than my own father. Perhaps it was easier to have compassion and rapport with someone who wasn't your flesh and blood; perhaps you were too busy correcting, chastising, disciplining your own and trying to do right. I didn't find that the case with Eddie, but he didn't live long enough for me to discover which fatherly path I would have taken.

The part-time job I undertook as manager/handy-man didn't take up much of my time. Mr. Baum's brother came out one Saturday and took me around to all the tenants to introduce me as the new *Manager*, and everyone was genial and warm. The buildings were recently built, and there weren't many repairs which were necessary, and because I was now officially a member of the Baum Company (different from the Baum Legal Group), we had a telephone installed in our kitchen for necessary telephone calls from neighbors or either of the Mr. Baums. I marveled at our luck.

Lina and I settled into our home and felt decidedly fortunate. We walked together to our separate jobs each morning and talked about our future. We carefully and sparingly shopped for new household items, and I worked during my lunch time and whenever Mr. Kupper could spare me, on making furniture for our house. It was a larger apartment than we had a need for, but it turned out, later, to be a boon to us. Mr. Kupper was teaching me to drive on Saturday afternoons, and I was saving money to get an automobile. Lina and I didn't go out as often as we had, although we did try to see any new W.C. Field movies which were around, and we did plenty of window shopping up and down Archer Avenue. Lina was learning to bake and cook, and we invited friends over for dinners, played card games, and laughed. When the weather was pleasant, Lina and I would sit out in the backyard on kitchen table chairs and read, and if rainy, we stayed inside on the almost new sofa we brought from Hallie's Second-Hand Store. We were content.

The year 1929 was filled with both joy and horror. Chicago's own, Al Capone was always in the newspapers, and his court dates and escapades entertained Mr. Kupper who kept me updated on the happenings. When in May of that year, Mr. Capone was sent to jail, Mr. Kupper said, "Well, that's that," and began to concentrate on his second major interest: the Chicago Cubs Baseball Team. Their entrance into the World Series that year made him as happy as I'd ever seen him, and their loss in October made him just as sad. But the newspapers and talk through that October about the Stock Market and financial dealings soon overtook Mr. K's sorrow at the Cubs' loss. I didn't understand the Stock Market or what its October collapse would mean for the average person. I had never even put my saved money in a bank, but kept it under some extra blankets in the back of a closet in a wooden keepsake box I had carved. That was a wise thing for me to do, as it turned out.

Prices, it seemed to me, were always going up, and while there were only a few cents difference (in 1927, bread was 9 cents a loaf and in 1929, it was 10 cents; a dozen eggs in 1927 was 35 cents, but 45 cents two years later), the money Lina and I earned seemed to be spent faster. We were always careful, but over the next few years, in what was to be known as the "Depression", money was precious, earning it was difficult, and when, at the beginning of November, Lina, told me that our family would be expanding, I panicked.

***

While we were both excited about the new person who would arrive sometime in May, I felt a sickness in my heart when I thought about what might happen. I did not want to upset or worry Lina, but all I could think of was my three dead brothers and my own two sons. I knew the misfortunes and glitches which could occur, but said nothing. Lina went to a doctor who practiced out of the Garfield Park Hospital which was not that far away. I wanted Lina to go to the hospital to deliver the baby, and we discussed it.

"Tom, it's so expensive. Doctor Andrews said I am healthy and doing well. I asked about hiring a nurse-midwife from the hospital. He gave me a name and telephone number, and said she was excellent if I decided to do that. I am nervous about the *Twilight Sleep* which they give women who are delivering babies. I guess I'm just nervous about it all. I talked to Elenore Wagner in the next building, and her two children were born at home. She said she would be able to help. I just think we can't afford it."

We discussed the matter. I really wanted her to safely deliver the baby in the hospital. I had been saving money for an automobile and had a little over one hundred dollars hidden away in my wooden box. One day, without telling Lina, I visited the hospital and talked to someone in their business office and got some numbers. If Lina had the baby in the hospital, and there were no other complications, the entire week stay in a maternity ward would cost forty-five dollars. It was expensive, and would take half my auto savings, but I didn't care. When I went back home, we talked again.

It was the end of January, and Lina was finished working. Her pregnancy was beginning to show and it was time to leave the office. I was glad she was home because I worried about her walking back to the apartment in her condition. While I was able to walk her to her job each morning, our quitting times were different, and she was home before me. The weather was unpredictable because it was winter. And Chicago. As February began, she would be safely at home, and I was relieved.

"I have the money, Lina, "and really, it's the safest thing to do. Let's plan on the hospital for you and the baby, and don't worry about the cost. I need to know that you are both safe."

She looked at me and smiled. "OK, Tom, but I want to talk to the nurse-midwife anyway. I know you have been saving that money for your car, and I feel bad about using it."

"Don't," and I smiled. "There's nowhere to go right now, and I can't think of a better way to spend it. I need to have you and our son or daughter safe," and while I claimed I didn't care if we had a girl or a boy, I wished for a daughter. I thought a girl would be stronger. At least, I hoped so.

We had to be careful about spending, and not just because mine was the only income we had once Lina was at home. During that year and the following ones, strange things happened. Things didn't cost as much. A loaf of bread dropped to eight cents and a dozen eggs to eighteen cents. That is, if you could get them. Prices may have dropped for a while, but so did job opportunities and salaries, and demand for items increased. I didn't understand it all. I was just hoping to hold on to my job. Mr. Kupper had numerous orders at the end of 1929… for bookcases, chairs, tables, and repairs were stacked up. But by the middle of 1930, many of the orders were cancelled, and while we did fill some of them, and complete the repairs, collecting the money owed was difficult. People just didn't have it. I waited it out. I told him I would take a pay cut, and then I did. He said I could use up the wood stacked in the shop to make furniture for the baby, so I accepted that as partial payment. He was worried, and so was I. I was grateful for the reduced rent we paid, and kept up the repairs on the three buildings. The Baum brothers seemed to be doing alright, although Lina found out that half the women in the office were let go because of budget tightening. Everyone was waiting out the Depression, reassured by those in power from President Hoover to Chicago's Mayor Thompson, and when they changed to President Roosevelt and Mayor Cermak and then Mayor Kelly, they all said the same thing. And blamed each other. And it was during this time, this depressing time, that my children were born.

***

Lina and I planned for a hospital birth once her labor started. Doctor Andrews thought the baby was due sometime during the week of May 18. Neither Lina nor I thought she would go into labor any earlier, and the doctor said that first babies are notoriously late. This one was early.

It was Thursday, May 1, and a beautiful spring day. Lina had gotten larger and was moving slower, but she was not one to complain, and when she was up early that morning, making coffee and packing my lunch, I didn't think there would be any problem.

"Feeling OK?" I asked her.

"Tired, and a backache, but otherwise, I'm fine. Elenore Wagner and I thought we would push little Essie in her stroller and walk to the market today. That's the only thing I have planned. I need to check the prices on hamburger meat and get some potatoes," and she straightened out my jacket. "Soon it will be too warm for this," and she kissed me as I left to walk to the shop. I was just finishing up a rocking chair for her and the baby and thought I might be able to get it home before the weekend if Mr. Kupper would loan me his car to transport it.

It was about three in the afternoon, and I was working on the final bit of staining I had to do on the rocker, thinking it would be dry and ready for tomorrow, when Mr. Kupper came in to the back and called me to the telephone. It was Mrs. Wagner.

"Thomas, please come home. When I came over to your apartment this morning, Lina was in labor. She didn't think things would proceed so quickly, and there was no time to get her to the hospital. She asked me to call the nurse-midwife, and she is here now, but things are happening quickly. Lina is asking for you."

The memory of Ava came to mind, and I told Elenore Wagner I was on my way immediately. Mr. Kupper closed the shop doors, and we got into his car, and again, I thought of the drive that Mr. Turner and I took, and what we found when we arrived there. I didn't think I could survive if Lina and my child did not.

When I ran into the house and into the bedroom where Lina was suffering, I watched as this baby came into the world accompanied by screams and blood and puke. I had not known a birth could be so violent, and the thought of another suffering child made me wonder whether drowning it in the same manner my father used to drown the kittens on the farm would not be a kinder and more humane way of dealing with the scene. This proved unnecessary. As the nurse and Elenore Wagner helped bring our daughter into the world, I marveled at the strength and power of Carolina Becker Allerton. A final push granted the baby freedom, and as the aftereffects of the birth were dealt with by the nurse, Elenore cleaned and wrapped the squalling child and placed her into Lina's arms.

Elenore looked at me, and said, "Go on, Thomas, see your wife and daughter. She's fine, and I'll go call the doctor. He was delivering another baby and could not get here. Go on, now. I'll take care of the telephone call."

I moved next to Lina who was laughing and crying and sweating all at once. She looked down at the child in her arms. Smiling, she looked at me. "Here, Thomas, hold Clara. She looks like you," and my wife named our daughter after my mother, and I was overwhelmed with gratitude.

Chapter 20   1890

Miss Daisy Winslow heaped the last of the wood into the large heating stove so it would be warm when the students came in. It was eight o'clock in the morning, and although the sun was shining, it was still chilly even though spring was close and the snow was gone. She expected a full schoolhouse today since the older boys were still in attendance and would be for a few weeks more until the spring farming began and they were needed at home. Miss Winslow thought that when Henry Ranking and Tim Walker arrived at the schoolhouse, she would send them to collect additional firewood from the Horton's farm, since it was their month to provide. Those boys were strong and reliable eighth graders, and she could count on them to help. If they didn't show, or only one did, she supposed she could send the Allerton boy, but she knew that sending him would be for her sake. If he were gone for an hour or so, there would be some semblance of order in the class. That child was only ten years old, but he was a handful, and although this was her second-year teaching, she knew she lacked the ability to handle recalcitrant students. After all, she was just nineteen years old herself.

She washed the slate board which ran across the front of the classroom, swept out the floor and, trying not to look, emptied the mousetrap which had caught one of the creatures who was trying to stay warm during the night. She had to do that because the Allerton boy had a terrible habit of teasing the girls with dead mice, especially Clara Hampton because he was sweet on her. Miss Winslow straightened the slates on the shelf and dusted the furniture and her desk. She opened the large *Webster's Dictionary* to the *M* section in preparation for the spelling bee. Once a week, she would take two grades together and give the students in those grades ten words to learn. A spelling bee would be held at the week's end, and today was Friday. She completed her tasks, then sat down close to the stove to wait. Soon she heard the noise of children gathering outside. She would ring the first bell in fifteen minutes, and then the second bell at exactly nine o'clock, five minutes later. She signed and drew her thin shawl closer thinking that at the end of the month when she would collect her wage of thirty-five dollars, some of it needed to be put away for the next winter when she would purchase a new shawl, a warmer one.

It was a few minutes later when she heard the first group of children outside the door. Someone knocked on the door, and she ignored the first knock, but when it persisted and she heard a voice (Sally

Jenkins?) call her name continually, she stood up and walked to the door pulling the shawl closer. She opened the door to look out. It was the first grader, Sally Jenkins, and she was in tears.

"Miss Winslow," and the little girl wiping her face, "Gid Allerton took my lunch pail and said he was going to eat my lunch and I won't have anything to eat," and fresh tears started.

Miss Winslow looked around the school yard and saw the boy hiding behind a tree holding the tin syrup bucket which held Sally's lunch. She stepped out onto the top step and pointed to him. "Come here right now with that, or you will be inside during both recesses today!"

The boy looked around the tree and decided that the punishment was more severe than he was willing to endure, so he came to the steps and handed the bucket back to Sally who grabbed it and turned her head into Miss Winslow's skirt, clutching the bucket to her chest.

"Here," he said, "I was only teasing," and he looked up at his teacher, "I just wanted to make sure she wouldn't drop the old bucket and lose her lunch. Wasn't going to keep it."

Miss Winslow stared at the boy and didn't say anything knowing he would simply backtalk. She knew his story, his background, and part of her felt sorry for him. She also knew that during the next few months, she would be boarding with his grandparents, the Allertons. It was their turn to keep her, to offer her room and board, and she would be with this child all day. She would try and adjust to him, and perhaps, she would be able to help him. At least to help him with his schoolwork. He wasn't stupid, just inattentive. He even showed sparks of great intelligence in the area of arithmetic. In fact, the last two ciphering matches were won by him. He even beat Henry Ranking, the eighth grader who was excellent with numbers. Miss Winslow sighed. This teaching job was more difficult than she thought it would be.

She took Sally's hand and took her inside the school building with her. They walked over to the long shelf upon which the children would place their lunch buckets, and she placed Sally's there. Miss Winslow helped her take off and hang up her coat, and said, "Sally, would you mind dusting my desk? That would be helpful. I'm going to ring the bell now."

Sally smiled and said, "Yes, Ma'am," and proceeded to dust the already dusted area while Miss Winslow took the bell from her desk and opened the door.

She stood at the door, ringing the bell and greeted the students as they entered. When the Allerton boy walked by her, she motioned him to her side and kept him there until the second bell was rung. Both Henry and Tim were present today, and she asked them to place their lunch buckets on the shelf and keep their coats on for the trip to collect the needed firewood. She looked at the boy next to her and said, "Now go in and hang up your things and be seated. Let's not have any additional problems today."

The Allerton boy did as he was instructed. He didn't want to get into additional trouble. He was aware that the teacher would soon be staying with him and his grandparents, and whatever he did in school would be discussed at each evening's supper. He was dreading that time. He also thought that there would be no chances for him to skip school and go to the pond instead, or talk his grandfather into allowing him to stay with him and help with the wood projects. He didn't like school. He only went because he had to, and he looked forward to finishing grade six so that he would be old enough to quit. His grandmother said she wanted him to complete all eight grades and receive the certificate which declared his accomplishment. But he didn't see the use of it. He would remain on the farm and learn from his grandfather and work in the woodshop, and the certificate wouldn't help with any of that.

He placed his own lunch pail on the shelf, hung up his coat and hat, and walked to his seat. He took the long way around so he could pass Clara's seat and knock her elbow. The only advantage to being too young to quit school yet is that he was able to see Clara most days. She had pretty, dark hair, and even though she lived in town, at least once a week, he walked her home, talking to her and telling her about fishing at the pond and collecting the eggs from the chickens, and bragging about the many wood carvings he was learning to make.

He had decided that the next time he and Pa walked the woods to look for green wood or large pieces of soft wood for carving, he would look for the special piece of wood which he would carve into the shape of a cat. He knew Clara liked them because she talked about the kitten she would have once her neighbor's cat birthed the next litter. He wasn't fond of the animals, but wanted to impress her with the gift he planned to make for her.

He moved into his seat and tried to pay attention to Miss Winslow. He had started the day badly and didn't want to get into more trouble, so when the class was instructed to take their slates out and practice their penmanship sentences, he looked at the large slate blackboard and, with a glance to Clara, began to copy them.

Chapter 21   1930+

When a very tall building begins to tumble down, to collapse, the people at the bottom will be flattened, but not immediately. Flattened nevertheless. That was the world in the 1930's. That was the United States. That was everyone we knew. Lina and our family, the people in the Baum's two-story buildings, the friends gathered around us survived, in part because we watched the top floors of the building come down around us, and we prepared the best way we could.

Joseph Kupper could not hold on to his business, and at the end of 1930, he sobbed as, together, we closed the shop and the business he had spent his adult life creating. The last thing we took down was the handmade wooden sign he insisted on keeping and took home to hang in the dining room of his house where he and Mrs. Kupper, who was not pleased with the redecoration, could view it daily. Lina and I kept in touch with the Kupper family, and Clara viewed them as the grandparents she did not have. After this, I was out of work.

I did whatever I had to do to bring in money. I found side jobs here and there. The construction business suffered greatly during the Depression, and while there was little work for carpenters, every now and then, Mr. Kupper would call me and tell me where I could pick up a job for a week or two. He had many contacts from over the years, and was always willing to tell anyone what a good worker, a dependable and competent carpenter I was. The little money I earned helped. Sometimes I took a job at a restaurant when a dishwasher was needed. A couple times, when the cook didn't show up, I grilled some hamburgers and made scrambled eggs for the customers. A gourmet chef I wasn't, but I helped when needed and happily took the extra cash. When, in 1932, the government's unemployment insurance started, I stood in line for the weekly cash payments. I swallowed my pride, along with the other dozens of men who lined the block, and then, when it was offered again, I stood in line again.

The Baum Legal firm asked Lina if she would be willing to take on some typing at home if they set her up with a typewriter. They too had scaled down their office workers to a skeleton crew. Lina was paid per page, and little Clara became used to the clinking noise as Lina typed rapidly during her naps. She was happy Mr. Baum had remembered her and glad to add something to our cash flow. And then there was Sandy, Lina's former roommate.

At the beginning of 1932, Sandy came over to spend some time with Lina and Clara. Her current roommate was leaving to go back home to Michigan because she had lost her job. While Sandy was still working, she could not find another girl who could afford to split the rent with her, and she couldn't manage it on her own. We ended up renting our third bedroom to Sandy, and while she couldn't pay us much, the monthly rent we charged her helped to pay ours which had gone up over the years. Not much, but a dollar was a dollar. Sandy loved Clara, and she was company for Lina on those evenings I had a side job or was washing dishes or on those long afternoons which turned into evenings at the unemployment line.

I was able to put my farming skills to use. I talked to Mr. Baum's brother, Mr. Gerald Baum, and got permission to use the backyards of the buildings for something other than poorly grown grass. I gathered the tenants of the three Baum buildings, and discussed the plan to plant vegetable gardens in the yards, and told them I would need their help, but I knew how to hoe and rake and plant and harvest, and if they were willing to lend a hand, we could have fresh vegetables for at least part of the year. The first year's crop was not very good, but in the late summer of 1933, there was a bumper crop of vegetables, and I proudly took a basketful to Mr. Baum and then dropped some off for the Kuppers.

The year 1933 was also the year our second child was born. This time, there was no discussion of Lina entering the Garfield Park Hospital. That hidden car fund money had been used up, and we scrapped together enough to pay the couple doctor visits she had and the cost for the nurse-midwife. Our son arrived in August, and when I saw he was healthy and safe, I again, felt gratitude. We named him Jan Joseph Allerton, after Lina's brother and Mr. Kupper, and called him *Joey*. We were crowded in the apartment with the two children and Sandy, but I didn't mind. There was something of a communal spirit. Neighbors helped each other, and we all made do with little because no one had much.

In the early autumn of 1933, on a night I didn't have any place to be, and after the children were in bed, Lina and I sat out in the back looking at the garden and talking. Sandy came out to tell us she was going to meet a friend for a walk, and we watched as she went out the back gate and down the street.

"I think her friend is a man," said Lina, "She's been quiet about it, but I believe it's serious."

"Not sure we could fit another person in this house," I joked.

Lina laughed. "If it's who I think it is, he has his own place, so there is no worrying about that, but we'd miss her rent money. I suppose that's an awful thing to say."

"Maybe," and I took her hand, "but we'll make it," and we talked about when times would get better, when I would have a real, full-time job, when we could save some money. I still wanted a car. Lina and I talked about taking the little ones and traveling so they could experience different places and view unfamiliar sights. We looked forward to those times, to better times.

***

I thought that one day, I would take my family to Levett, Illinois, to the small town where I was born. I hope it's still there. I want to take Lina and Clara and Joey around the town to see the post office and general store and hardware store, the church, the schoolhouse. We'll travel out to the farm where I lived and worked, if it's still intact. I would like them to see the woodshop and the chicken coop and the house where I grew up, where I left my dying father, although I won't tell the children that. I haven't told Lina that part of my life yet. I will, before we travel there. She should know the last part that I am keeping to myself.

We will park the car…the one I saved for…and walk out to the wooded area and look for the large stones I placed on top of Molly's grave. I'll tell my children about the dog and how I tramped with her through these woods and how, on the cold winter nights, when I was lonely, she curled up on the end of my bed and slept with me. When Clara and Joey beg to get a dog of their own, I'll agree and say that once we get home, we'll look for one, but they will need to care for it, and I'll teach them how. Perhaps we'll name the dog *Molly*.

We'll walk to the small family gravesite where my other family, the one I never knew, is buried. I'll point out the initialed stones of my great-grandparents and grandparents. I'll show them my great-aunt Dorothy's grave. I'll read the names of my brothers: *Son, 1901, Edward, 1902, Edward 1903,* and point out that the last Edward is the twin brother I never knew. My mother's stone will be there, and I wonder if next to it I will see another stone engraved with the name *Gideon Allerton*. I believe I will. I'll knee down, in the same way I knelt at Eddie's grave, and whisper my apology to my father. I'll show Clara and Joey how to pull the large weeds from around the stones, and if crabapples have fallen on top of the graves, we'll remove them, and when we leave, the graves will be cleaned until the next visit.

And when we walk back to the car, after everyone gets in, I'll stand and look back at the woods and see the trees, and remember the lessons: how to consider the grain, the changes in moisture, differences and varieties in sawn boards, the complexities of joinery, the uses of hardening oil, varnishes, and wax blends, the tools, safety considerations, cleanliness. I'll think about how the work brought comfort to me then and how it still does. And when Clara and Joey begin to fuss, and they will, I'll get into the car, smile at Lina, and drive us home. Some day.

Chapter 22   1887

Gideon rubbed the sandpaper against the casket exactly the way his grandfather had taught him. This was a lengthy process in the late summer heat, but he wanted to do it correctly. He admired his grandfather, and in his young mind, he had become aware that his grandparents were now his parents. He didn't remember the funeral of his mother because he had been two-years-old, but his father's funeral was just last year when he was six, and the memory of that day was crisp. He thought about it for a while, and then stopped because the sadness started to overwhelm him. He concentrated on the sanding. The smoothness he was creating made him smile. Old Mrs. Tanner had died, and this casket would be used for her burial, so he was diligent about his assignment and watchful with his work.

"Grandpa, I think this is done. Do you want to see it?"

Tomas Allerton walked over to examine the efforts of his grandson and nodded. "That's good, Gid. Just a few more rubs and you can stop. You're understanding this work and getting better at it." He stood and watched the boy make the sweeping movements he had taught him to make, and then glanced at his pocket watch. "Time for me to get along. Going to wash up and get my jacket. When I come back, you can help lift it into the wagon."

The man left the boy to continue the sanding, and Gid finished the last spot on the edge before he stood back to admire his work. When the grandfather returned, he was wearing his dark coat, the one one he kept for the sad business. He walked over to the horse and wagon and moved it to the out-building used as his workshop. Once there, he maneuvered the finished casket into the back, adjusting it correctly. Of course, the boy didn't help much, but he tried. Once the casket was placed, an old blanket was thrown on top and tied down to protect the box from the dross of flying birds while it was transported to its woeful destination.

"Grandpa, can I go with you? I could help."

Tomas climbed to the front wagon seat and looked at his grandson, so like his own dead son at that age, so remindful of the son who had the misfortune to imbibe until the sipping became swallowing and then gulping. The son who swilled more at the death of his young wife and left this child to wander and be disregarded until the grandparents took pity on the boy and brought him to their home. This grandson who had become a son.

"Not this time, Gid. When you are older, I might need your help, but for now, this business is mine. Some day."

"Well, how long will you be? Will we be able to go fishing today like we planned?"

The pond was not far from their farm, and over the past spring and summer months, Gid and his grandfather had walked there and spent time trying to catch the contained fish. The pond was large and rumored to house largemouth bass and channel catfish which could be caught if you knew the right place to set your pole. Gid hadn't caught anything yet, but he enjoyed the adventure and liked to watch for the reclusive, solitary mud-turtle who dwelled in the pond

"I should be back in a couple hours. We can spend some time at the pond then. Meantime, Granny can use you in the kitchen where she is baking those molasses cookies you like. Go on in and wash up. I'll be back soon," and Tomas clicked his tongue and called to the horse to, "Git now," and the wagon moved.

As the wagon pulled forward, Tomas reviewed his obligations. The town did not yet have a replacement undertaker, so he, town carpenter, had taken over the task of building caskets: eternity boxes for the burial of deceased citizens. He had built his own son's last year. He helped his sobbing wife to line the wooden box with the coffin quilt she had originally prepared for herself. They lifted Edward's body into the casket, and Tomas sent his wife into the house while he nailed it shut. His neighbor showed up to help lift the box onto the back of the wagon, and a small procession traveled to the family burial site at the end of the wood, near the copse of crabapple trees, where Dorothy Allerton, Edward's younger sister, rested. The grandson was held on his grandmother's lap as she sat next to her husband who had clicked his tongue and told the horse to "Git now".

As temporary undertaker, Tomas would help carry the casket to the bedroom where Mrs. Tanner's body was laid out after being washed and shrouded by her two daughters and her daughter-in-law. He would dismiss the women and ask for one or two of the men to help lift and place the deceased into the box which would then be carried into the parlor to rest, watched over by family, until burial in the town cemetery the following day. Given Mrs. Tanner's old age and lack of flesh, Tomas assumed only one other man would be needed for the lifting chore. Afterwards, he would stand for a bit in respectful silence, head lowered in dissembled prayer, because he stopped adhering to that particular principle years ago, and in time, would shake hands and articulate his condolences. On his way out, the last man to shake his hand would place the expected fee into it and thank him. Then he would travel back to Gideon and spend time with him at the pond.

During the hours his grandfather was gone, Gideon was in the kitchen with his grandmother. He was not as helpful as he was talkative, but Granny did not mind. She had always wanted additional children, but only had the two. When her daughter, Dorothy, drowned at five-years-old, she placed all her love, care, and attention into the raising of her son, Edward, cuddling, and kissing him constantly. Perhaps, she often wondered at the early morning hours when sleep eluded her, one could love too much. Years later, she remained devastated at her additional loss, and was determined not to spoil this boy, Edward's son, so she let him talk and she answered, but hugged him measuredly only at night before he fell asleep in the wooden bed her husband had made for their son. She was wary of her actions, distrustful of her feelings, watchful about her sentiments. She had lost her two children. This one needed protecting, and if that meant curtailing her responses and reactions to him, then that is what she would do.

"Granny, if I catch some fish today, can we eat them for supper tonight?"

Mary Allerton finished moving the cookies from the baking tin and placed them on the table as she answered, "That would be fine, Gid. And if you aren't lucky enough to catch one today, we can have the stew from yesterday. And cookies afterwards. I suppose you want to try one now?"

"Can I?"

"Take one that is cooled from over there," and she pointed to the back of the table.

Gideon sat and chewed his cookie and watched his grandmother work. He preferred being with his grandfather, but while he waited for his return, the cookies were the perfect distraction. As the baking continued, the boy chewed and looked about the kitchen. He had spent so much of his short life with his grandparents that he could hardly remember another kitchen. He took one more cookie when his grandmother's back was turned and thought about what he would ask her.

"Granny, tell me about my name again."

"Your name? Land sakes, Gid, you know about it."

"Please tell it again. I like to hear it."

"Well, when your grandfather went to war, your Pa and his sister, Dorothy, and I were left alone on the farm. Times were hard, and we needed protecting. The war was a mean time, and we never knew if the fighting would come our way. Grandpa's uncle came to stay with us and help out as he was too old to fight. He spent time with your Pa."

"Did Grandpa do fighting?"

"I suppose he had to. That part you'll need to ask him."

"And that uncle's name was the same as mine. Right?"

"It was. He was Uncle Gideon, and your Pa really took to him, and they did the things you and your grandpa do. They fished, and walked the woods, and talked, and Uncle Gideon taught your Pa how to whistle and carve."

"And that's why I was named *Gideon*. Right?"

"Yes, it is. Your Pa loved his Uncle Gideon and named you after him. People do that to help remember."

Gideon sat back and finished chewing. He thought about the father he was beginning to forget, and the old uncle he never met. He wondered at the power and sanction of names. He considered a plan and made a decision.

"Granny, I think that if I have a son someday, I know what I'll name him."

Mary finished the last of the cookies. She turned to him and wiped her hands on her apron as she looked at the boy.

"And what will that be, Gideon?"

"Tomas. If I have a son, I'll name him Tomas."

Mary stood still for a while thinking and then nodded. Breaking her own rule, she walked over to the grandson she was trying not to spoil with love, and while saying, "That's a good plan, Gid," she hugged him.

Chapter 23   **1865**

Traveling from the small village of Levett which was just north of Champaign in Champaign County, Illinois to Camp Butler in Sangamon County, just east of Springfield, was an arduous trip on horseback. A good rider with an excellent horse could do it in four days with stops for rest, water, and human and animal needs. Tomas Allerton managed it in three days. When he entered the grounds of the camp and found the sign-up tent for volunteers, he was cursorily examined, deemed fit for duty, given his uniform, supplies, and assigned to the volunteer barracks of the Union Army. By 1863, the management of the Union's volunteer army was logical and ordered and planned. Tomas knew he would need to undergo the company drilling, the skirmish drilling, and the dress parade drilling that all volunteers were required to complete daily. He assumed that because he had brought his own horse along and was a proficient rider and handler of the animal, he would be chosen for the calvary, sent there for training, and then appointed to fight in a southern state. That is what he envisioned. What he wanted. He did not anticipate what happened.

Camp Butler was not just a training facility for Union soldiers. In 1862, it had also become a prison for captured Confederate soldiers, and not all of them survived to be traded for Union prisoners. Scurvy, dysentery, pneumonia, along with crudely treated war wounds kept many of the Confederate soldiers from returning to their homes. Instead, poor sanitation, inadequate food, and rampant disease helped to fill the burgeoning cemetery which, of necessity, was created behind the barracks and tents, and hospital building that formed the camp. And when Tomas Allerton's skill as a carpenter became known, his horse was reallocated, and he was assigned to remain at Camp Butler as a medic. After all, cutting boards for caskets or cutting off gangrenous limbs were similar, and Tomas did both.

He had volunteered, having left his wife and young son and baby daughter in the care of his uncle, Gideon Allerton, and would fulfill his promise and vow of loyalty to the Union. When, in the spring of 1865, as the Civil War ended and the dead president was mourned, Camp Butler was dismantled and the remaining soldiers were sent home. The cemetery endured, becoming harbor for both Confederate and Union soldiers slumbering under prairie greenery in cohesive quietude.

Tomas Allerton walked home. He kept company with other soldiers traveling the same direction, and as they arrived where they were going, or just stopped walking, farewells were given, and the men, tired from fighting, worn out from pain and disease and poor food and trauma, went about life, trying to regain a sort of normality. Tomas was no different. He finally made it home to his wife, who when she saw him limping down the road fell to the ground sobbing, and to his children, who avoided the father they didn't remember. Tomas was helped into his house by Uncle Gideon who assisted him in bathing and cleaning and dressing in his old clothes which were much too large for his emaciated frame. In the meanwhile, his wife, Mary, cooked eggs and toasted bread, and slathered homemade blackberry jam on the pieces which Tomas quickly ate and promptly threw up. Such richness in food was a gradual adjustment for him.

For months after the homecoming, Tomas slept fourteen hours a day or more. Mary tried to keep baby Dorothy occupied and quiet while she went about the house and farm duties, and Uncle Gideon took Eddie out to fish in the pond and walk the woods. Eventually, Tomas regained some of his strength and most of his sanity, and began to work again on the small farm and in his woodshop. Normality took years to achieve and when it came, its form had become mystifying and confounding.

Summer seemed to take hold and last through October of that year, and that pleased Eddie whose favorite occupation was fishing at the pond with Uncle Gideon. This would be one of the year's last ventures. The leaves were snowflaking around them and the rocks they sat on as they flipped their lines into the water were much colder than before. But the sun, although not summer sultry, was congenial and mellow, and Eddie lifted his face to gather its kisses. They had packed some of the leftover bacon and biscuits from breakfast and planned to linger at the pond and in the woods until afternoon. Eddie and Uncle Gideon had enjoyed each other's fellowship for the years Tomas had been away, sawing boards and limbs in the service of the Union, and now that he was back, Eddie held a fear that his uncle would be gone.

"Uncle Gideon, what will happen now?"

The man pushed his hat back where it had been shading his eyes and looked at the boy. "What do you mean?"

"Now that Pa is home from the fightin', will you have to go back to Chicago?"

"Well, I'm not sure. I won't leave for a while yet, until your Pa is back on his feet and strong again. I'll be here through this fall and winter, and once next spring comes around, we'll see."

The boy watched the pond for a time. "I don't want you to leave."

"I like it here too, Eddie, but will only stay if I'm not in the way. No one thought this war would last so long. Figured your Pa would be gone for a couple months at most, and then he'd be back home. Anyway, right now I have a mind to eat one of them biscuits with some bacon. Throw some here."

Eddie placed his fishing rod, the one whittled for him by Uncle Gideon, down and reached into the sack behind him. He took out two biscuits, placing some of the cold bacon on top, and bending over, gave them to the uncle. He took some for himself, and they chewed in unison and were quiet. Eddie dusted his hands of the crumbs and reached back into the sack for the jar of water. He unscrewed the top and offered it first to the adult who waved it away, so Eddie took a long swallow. He watched as Uncle Gideon reached into his breast pocket and pulled out a flask which he unscrewed and put to his lips for a long, hard swig. Then he wiped the back of his hand against his mouth and sighed.

Eddie looked over and spoke. "Can I have a drink?"

Uncle Gideon let out a roar. "Ha! I'd catch all kinds of blazes letting a five-year-old drink!"

"I'm almost six."

"Makes no mind, boy. Your Pa, peaked or not, would wallop my hide. There'd be a smart chance of that."

Eddie turned to his pole and picked it up again. "Well, I'd like to taste it sometime."

"Those times will come when you are grown a bit. And don't go tellin' your Ma about this."

"I never have," replied Eddie, and then tried once more. "I just want a taste. Does it taste good?"

Uncle Gideon pulled in his line and examined it before answering. "It's an acquired taste, boy. More than that, it sometimes feels good."

They sat still in the fading afternoon sun. Leaves flew down, and despite the shine, a chill was spreading around them.

"No fish today. Think they're settling at the bottom for winter," and the uncle pulled out his pocket watch. "Let's pack it in and begin to walk back. We can travel the long way back through the woods and look for the right pieces for the whittling."

Eddie was looking forward to being taught to whittle and perhaps to carve. Last year when he had just turned five, he was gauged too young to hold a sharp knife. But this year, at winter, they planned to sit around the fire, and he would take lessons from his uncle. He wanted to carve a doll for his sister and a keepsake heart for Ma. He wasn't sure, what, if anything he could make for his Pa. He didn't know him yet.

The two of them stood up, and Uncle Gideon stretched out his back and shrugged his shoulders which were growing arthritic with age. They picked up their poles and the sack with the remains of lunch, and without talking, without needing to, they turned away from the static pond and ambled into the trees, into the long path which led through the woods and around to the farm.

They would wander through the timbers, looking for the proper wood, collecting some of the best pieces to bring home, to add to their growing pile in the basket near the fireplace. They would roam for a time, and once they reached the crabapple trees bordering the edge of the farm property, they could observe the farmhouse. On the porch, little Dorothy and Ma and Pa, having just gotten up from another nap, would be occupying the porch swing, moving gently, watching for the wanderers.

They shuffled through the leaves on the path; Eddie trying to step in synch with his great-uncle. As Uncle Gideon reached into his breast pocket for the flask, Eddie began to whistle the way the uncle had taught him. The diminishing sun formed mottled shadowmarks through the trees, and for a while, thoughts of war and pain and leaving and chores and agonies yet to come vanished as tranquility penetrated and contentment settled.

Acknowledgements

Thank you to…

Pierre and Vivian for their advice and help;

Bill for his expertise in important matters;

Amy, my French-speaking friend;

The team (listed in order of age): K.M., A.S., J.G.;

And much gratitude to the *Captain*…you know who you are…

Some cause happiness wherever they go;
others whenever they go.

Oscar Wilde

Excerpt from *Her Cousin Julia*

Chapter 1   **Deciding**

No matter how often Julia begged her cousin to kill her, June refused.

"Stop that nonsense," June would say, "there is nothing wrong with you. We are the same age. and you are in better shape than me, and I intend to continue living and enjoying life."

Julia snorted in derision. "Of course. You have something to live for. You have children and grandchildren, and a group of friends you visit and work out with, and I have no one. Arnie is dead, and I never had children and my friends, if you can call them that, are also gone. Moved away. Never call or visit. And the ones who do only do so because they think I'll leave them jewelry or money when I'm dead, which I won't. I'll leave it all to you, June. I'll go to the lawyer and amend my will today if you will kill me tomorrow."

June glanced sideways at her cousin, refusing to answer her, and continued to read her book club's next selection. This was a tired harangue. Julia was being ridiculous again, and she didn't mean what she said. She got into these moods and said the wildest things. Suggested insane ideas. It made June regret the move she had agreed to years ago.

Three years ago, Julia suggested that since they were both widows and aging, they combine their households and move together to the Winchester Senior Complex. It sounded logical and reasonable then, and June, knowing that her children had their own lives and families, agreed to Julia's plan. The townhouse was large: six rooms, two bathrooms, and a large outside space. The monthly HOA assessment took care of the lawn work and snow removal, and except for the three to enter the townhouse, there were no stairs to climb. The connecting wall to their neighbor was in the garage so they were never bothered by any noise from Mr. Simmons who was, by nature, a quiet person anyway. The Winchester townhouse was in all respects, perfect.

A plethora of groups and activities were available for the residents, and June took full advantage of them. Julia did not. She could have, and did attend a few meetings for various groups, but found the people, as she complained to June, *trite* and *insipid*. Those were her words, and she didn't return a second time to any activities. She stayed in the townhouse, watching television, and complaining to June whenever she was around. June enjoyed the clubs and activities, and Julia's petulance was encouragement to continue being active. But it was early in the day, and June was still at home, at least for another hour. She was meeting a friend at the exercise room where they were going to join the new group that was starting: Senior Shape-Up. Julia had refused to go.

"*Senior Shape-Up?* No thanks. A bunch of old ladies flapping their arthritic, fatty arms and legs around! Not for me. Why do you want to go? Who are you getting in shape for? Really June, you have the stupidest ideas."

Julia, for all her non-movement, was in decent shape for a seventy-three-year-old. She had always tended to be on the thin side. June was not thin, and she resented the reference to fatty arms and legs, because hers were. But she knew this was typical of Julia's barbed comments and chose to ignore it. She had dealt with her cousin all her life, and knew her commentary mandated ignoring.

June's father and Julia's mother had been siblings. The cousins were born a few months apart and lived near each other although in vastly different houses. Julia's mother had married a wealthy man and their house was large and expertly decorated, and the family wanted for nothing. And that was saying something because the cousins were born in 1930, the early days of the Depression. June's family resided in a small apartment. Her father married for love and had trouble holding a job even in the best of economic times, so *want* was a constant visitor. She slept in a miniscule bedroom which was a made-over storage space, and jealously arose as Julia lorded her large room and many toys over her cousin. Julia's mother and June's mother had been classmates in high school, so the two families were together often and the cousins were routinely in each other's company because they were only children. Given their past, June thought she should be used to Julia's grumpiness and grousing, but it was becoming harder and harder to take.

Julia glanced at June and questioned, "Did you call the maintenance office about the bushes in back?" Julia thought the back foliage was overgrown and needed trimming. She wouldn't call herself because June was her unofficial secretary and was expected to take care of such details, a tacit agreement given the money Julia regularly put out. However, the bushes had been trimmed just over a month ago, and June knew there was no sense in calling.

"Julia, they were just trimmed and are fine. I'm sure they will be done again in the fall," and June closed her book and sighed. She got up to refill her coffee cup and looked out the back. It would become warm, but right now it looked pleasant, and she thought she would sit outside for a bit. Away from Julia.

"Coffee again? I HATE the smell, and after all these years, you should know that. Heat up the water for my tea. Really, June, I think you should drink tea instead. It's actually healthier, and if you avoid the milk you put in your coffee, you would lose some of that fat," and Julia reached over for the remote. It was time for her morning game show. She turned the kitchen's television on, adjusted the sound to LOUD, and proceeded to wind her way through the many channels her subscription money afforded them. June rarely watched anything. She stayed busy with other activities.

Making Julia's tea was a long process. While the filtered water heated, June reached into the cupboard and removed the tin of expensive imported loose tea from the Harrington Tea Company and placed it on the table in front of Julia along with the specially ordered Manuka honey from New Zealand (said to have special healing properties). A spoon, special tea strainer, and a lovely imported tea cup and saucer were set there also. The thinly sliced lemons came on another matching plate and Julia arranged her tea to be seeped for no more than four minutes. She timed everything carefully and then poured the tea, added the swirl of honey, and topped it off with a thin lemon slice. She would stir once with the spoon, then set it on the extra plate (it was gauche to place a teaspoon directly on the table), and take a delicate sip of the beverage.

June was used to waiting on her cousin in this way. It was an unspoken agreement because most of the money for the townhome and its furnishings and contents and utility bills and HOA payments and groceries and television cable came from Julia whose dead husband, Arnie, had been wealthy. June had married for love. Like her father. It was one of the reasons she had agreed to this living arrangement. She wasn't sure her measly pension and small social security check would cover her monthly bills. She sucked it up and for three years, she and Julia had lived together in the fine townhouse, affording June a financial freedom she would not have enjoyed.

"Is there anything else you want? I'm going to sit outside and read until time for the class. Are you sure you don't want to go with me? It would be good for you to get out and see some of the women. They ask about you."

"Humph," replied Julia, "They gossip about me, you mean. I hope you keep your big mouth closed and tell them nothing. No, I won't go, and no, there is nothing else I want just now," and Julia turned up the volume as her gameshow began. She was busy placing the tea strainer onto the matching plate (teabags were also gauche). She checked the time for exactly four minutes of seeping as she watched the program. June slipped out the lovely French doors which lead from the kitchen to the back where she seated herself on one of the soft cushioned patio furniture chairs. Julia had them specially made.

She put her coffee cup on the table to her side and opened her book. She had lost interest in reading but needed to get away from her cousin whose penetrating, squawking laughter could be faintly heard through the French doors. June often second-guessed her decision to live with her cousin. It wasn't easy and was becoming more difficult as the years went on. Being tethered to someone because of money was torturous, and the past three years had been particularly grueling. June looked over the carefully and expertly manicured small lawn to the impeccably trimmed small bushes. Across the way was the large two-story building which housed some offices, rental rooms, library, and the gym. The first-floor large exercise area was where she would go to flap around her fatty arms and legs, and to remove herself from the continuing comments, mostly nasty, of her cousin. At times like these, in the difficult mornings which were becoming more frequent, she questioned her decision about moving in with Julia. She was spending increased time reviewing their life together and wondering how much more she could take.

Behind her, in the kitchen, she heard Julia yell out incorrect answers to the televised questions and shout at the contestants that they were *dolts* and *idiots*, familiar terms to June. Her book lay open but June was not reading. She was thinking about the conversation from earlier. The one where Julia, once again, bemoaned her fate and her life. The once where she asked her cousin to do away with her. June was deciding. It would take care and planning and deliberation and more than a smidgeon of fortitude and bravery and luck, but as she stared ahead at the manicured lawn and the bushes that needed no additional trimming, she made a decision. June was going to kill her cousin Julia.